Dancing in the Storm

By Shelly Maguire and Beth Huffman

STANLEY PUBLISHING CO.

Dancing in the Storm

Copyright ©2012 by Shelly Maguire and Beth Huffman

All rights reserved. No part of this book may be used or reproduced in any manner whatsoever or by any electronic or mechanical means including information storage and retrieval systems without written consent from the publisher, except for brief quotations for reviews.

Original edition published in the United States by Stanley Publishing Company.
El Paso, Texas
www.stanleypublishing.com

Maguire, Shelly
Huffman, Beth
   Dancing in the Storm
ISBN 978-1-4675-2506-0

First printing 2012

Cover design by Rishi Arora
www.rishinealarora.com

Book design by Marsha Morris

Printed in the United States by 360 Digital Books
www.360digitalbooks.com

Acknowledgements

I would like to express my deepest gratitude to the many people who saw me through this book; to all those who provided support, exchanged ideas, read and re-read pages of rough drafts and who wrote and re-wrote pages in order to help me fulfill my dream.

First I would like to thank my co-author, Beth Huffman. Without her guidance, support and commitment to this project, I would have given up writing my life story. Her compassion, love and true caring ways have turned someone who was initially a stranger into a friend whom I now love dearly and call family. I will miss our long hours of skyping, laughing, crying and trading compliments. I would also like to thank her dear husband, Herb, for without his willingness to eat fast food and share his wife's time with me, we would not have finished this journey.

Thank you to my publisher, Marsha Morris, for taking an interest in our lives and our story. Without her, this book would never have found its way to press. Her generosity and kindness are so very much appreciated.

I want to thank my loving and devoted husband, Frankie, who has only seen the back of my head since I started writing this book. He has unselfishly supported and encouraged me all the way in spite of the time it took away from him. Without his love, there would not be a perfect ending to my book and a storybook beginning for the rest of my life. I love you.

Lastly, I want to thank my Mom, Dad and two sisters, Mindy and Lori. Without the support of my family, I would not have a story to tell. Their love, friendship, respect and kindness have made me the person I am today. Mom, thank you for demanding that we continue to check for misspelled words, editing my sentences which were too long and for reading my story 345 times in the process. I cannot express adequately in words how much I love you all.

My deepest appreciation goes to Dr. Light, Lisa, Bob, Jodi, Dr. Salathe, Dr. Campos and the entire CF team in West Palm for taking such great care of me. They have encouraged me when I am down, listened to my "what ifs" and "how abouts" and are available to me at a moment's notice when I'm not well.

Additional thanks goes to the Cystic Fibrosis Foundation for their commitment to finding a cure and their funding of research projects that have been responsible for the breakthroughs I've seen in my lifetime.

I sincerely appreciate all of my friends and family who contributed to my life story and book. I ask forgiveness of all those who have been with me over the course of the years and whose names I did not have space to mention. You remain in my heart and are dear to me.

Foreword

Two words come to mind when I think about Shelly: Inspiration and Adventure. She is what we call a "mover and a shaker," developing one idea that morphs into something else and from there seems to effortlessly come to fruition. How many people can say they have owned their own successful business, researched and developed a product for retail sales, sells it on national television with a presence that would paralyze most, and continues to expand?

It has always been so exciting to hear about "what's happening next" and yet, when you are with Shelly, you feel like YOU are the most important person in the world because she is so humble and selfless and has a sense of humor like none other. You forget that she has cystic fibrosis until her cough reminds you and if you ask about it, the focus turns to you and the insignificant cut on YOUR finger becomes more important!

Time passes very quickly when you're with Shelly because she has a gift of making life so fun for herself and everyone around her. I am confident that those who read her story will feel like they have known her forever. I consider myself blessed and privileged that I have.

With Love,

Robyn Cherry

To my loving family and husband

I love the smell of autumn filtering into our screened-in-porch tonight while writing some final thoughts of the day in my journal. I'm caught between the rewarding emotions of what has transpired the past few months and the magical wonder of what lies ahead. My childhood dream was to be an author and this dream has come true. I've written two books about beautiful human beings whose courage is beyond inspirational. Though I've been retired from teaching English for many years now, I feel like I've returned to the classroom in pursuing my passionate love for writing.

I've received inquiries from several people who have asked me to write books about their lives. Just today I received an intriguing email from a remarkable woman with whom I feel a connection somehow.

I am captivated by her message that begins…

The Emails

Hello Beth,

My name is Shelly Maguire. I am 51 years old and have cystic fibrosis. I have battled my disease since being diagnosed at the age of 9. I was told that I would be fortunate to celebrate my 18th birthday. Life has not been easy but it has shaped who I am. I know that we are only limited in life by our attitudes and the way we deal with any affliction or challenge. I have my own company called Ice Elements Skin Care (www.shellymaguire.com) and sell my products on HSN.

I have been doing live television shows there for the last seven years. I also have a consultant business, radio show and have done motivational speaking for businesses. Prior to that I owned numerous start-up businesses and franchises.

My dream has always been to help motivate others to challenge themselves in the face of any obstacle – not just CF. It may be weight loss, codependent relationships, business hardships and disease (all of which I have faced). I especially want to help children and young adults because I know as a child and teenager how hard it was being 'different.' I want to share my challenges, struggles and victories not as they relate to me but as they relate to others who have also faced difficulties.

I just read your book *Run, Amy, Run!* about your former student who battled CF. This is why I have contacted you. I've always wanted to write my story in order to encourage others to never give up. I have a saying above my desk that reads: 'I get knocked down but I get back up again.'

Would you consider helping me tell my story? I am in search of a great partner who could make my dream a reality, one that would raise thousands of dollars for CF research and other children's charities.

I appreciate your time and look forward to hearing from you.

Take care,
Shelly Maguire

~ ~ ~

Dear Shelly,

I would be honored to help you write your story. I will be calling you soon to share some ideas. I'm looking forward to watching your presentation live on HSN tomorrow.

Beth Huffman

~ ~ ~

How Can She Have CF?

I am in disbelief. How can Shelly be living with CF and look this healthy at 51 years of age?

The fact she has lived this long is a miracle in itself. Although there are individuals who live into their 40's and 50's with this disease, the median age of survival for a person with CF is in the late 30's.

How is it possible that she had the stamina to appear on HSN this morning promoting her skin care products? She never coughed once during her 15-minute presentation. This is unbelievable! People with CF are plagued with a deep persistent cough, one that often leaves them gasping for air. Yet she only cleared her throat twice; it was done so quietly I'm sure it went unnoticed by the TV viewers.

So many people with CF sound like their sinuses are extremely congested when they talk. Not Shelly. There is only a slight raspy sound to her voice; maybe it's irritation from coughing too hard for so many years. At the end of her last email she mentioned going for a run. How can this be? Many people living with CF who are half her age don't have the lung capacity to walk very far let alone run. Her trim, attractive stature suggests a strong-willed woman who runs to live.

I paid close attention when the camera zoomed in on her hands as she was applying skin cream to the models' faces. I leaned forward to see if her fingernails were noticeably rounded or clubbed, a common characteristic of people with cystic fibrosis. Even though they appeared slightly rounded, her fingernails were beautifully manicured and sculpted.

After several minutes of scrutiny, I quit looking for a woman living with cystic fibrosis. I couldn't find her. Instead I was mesmerized by Shelly's sheer professionalism as she moved with ease from one model to the next … like a graceful ballerina with impeccable poise. She made it look so easy; she made it look so fun. Many viewers probably found themselves envying this attractive, vivacious woman. Many were undoubtedly thinking, "What I would give to look like Shelly Maguire and live her life of luxury!"

A drama awaits. Why am I looking so forward to writing a book about someone I don't know?

Will I meet the Shelly Maguire who surely must struggle to breathe freely, a woman whose lungs have been held prisoner by her disease since birth? Or will I meet the professional Shelly Maguire who is always camera-ready and extremely driven to succeed? Maybe they are one in the same.

There is something about this woman whose persona is warm and sincere. She seems so real. If I were to follow my heart right now, I'd call her and say, "This is Beth Huffman, Shelly. I enjoyed watching your presentation on TV this morning. Would you like to come over for blueberry muffins and a cup of tea?" My instincts tell me she would say, "I love blueberry muffins! I'm on my way."

~ ~ ~

The First Phone Conversation

"Hello, Shelly? This is Beth Huffman."

"Beth, it's wonderful to hear you in person! I'm traveling in the car right now so I hope our connection is good."

"I can hear you perfectly. You sound just like you did on TV."

"Great. I want to start my book as soon as possible! Where do we begin? How will we write this together? I have Skype. Will that help?"

"I have Skype too. This will be invaluable in communicating. I'll learn so much about you just by interacting. The logistics of making this work will be challenging because you live in Florida, I'm in Ohio and my publisher is in Texas. We'll talk frequently on the phone and we'll need to exchange a mountain of emails. In fact, many of the emails we exchange will be in the book. You might want to warn your family that I'll need emails from them, too."

"No problem there. I'm so lucky. I have the best parents and sisters in the world. They'll provide all the information you need ... actually they'll provide too much information at times! I'll warn you now, Beth, there are chapters in my life I'm ashamed to talk about because I was so rebellious. I was awful. I acted out in anger and denial of my disease. Can we maybe skip those chapters?"

"No way! There is no 'skipping those chapters' allowed, Shelly Maguire."

"I was afraid you'd say that. Okay then. You're going to get the good, the bad and lots of ugly too! Where do you want me to start? I move quickly so I'll have an email to you in a few days.

Will that be soon enough?"

"That will be fine. I realize you move at lightning speed but it doesn't work that way in writing a book. I'll do my best to keep pace but why don't you see if they sell anything called, 'Slow Down Shelly' pills? Buy as many bottles as you can!"

"Hold on a second, Beth. I'm having trouble hearing you over my coughing. I apologize."

"Shelly, let's hang up. You're coughing so hard. We'll talk tomorrow."

"No, don't hang up. This happens all the time."

"That's what I couldn't understand when you were on HSN yesterday. You never coughed once. How was that possible?"

"It's the strangest thing. My family and I talk about this all the time. I always say a little prayer that I won't cough before I go on and so far I've been lucky."

"It sounds like you're choking. We seriously need to hang up."

"Please don't hang up yet. I just need a tissue because I'm coughing up a little bit of blood."

"What does that mean? Should you be finding the nearest hospital?"

"No. It could just be scar tissue from my lungs or signs of an infection. I'll be fine."

"If you aren't feeling up to writing your book, you'll tell me, won't you? Promise me."

"I promise. But that won't happen. I'm determined to tell my story. I'm going to help others. Nothing will stop me."

"We'll talk in a few days, Shelly. Hopefully you'll feel better."

"Thanks so much for calling, Beth. I think we're going to be great partners."

"Me too."

~ ~ ~

The Pied Piper

I met Shelly today. The long conversation via our computers was so comfortable and candid. I never dreamed how open she would be about her life so quickly. Her enthusiasm is contagious. She is like a Pied Piper who magically lures you into following her; I'm already devoted to following this charming free spirit in anticipation of an unforgettable journey.

It was immediately clear she is determined to tell her story in a big way. She wants her book to reach out to those struggling with CF and to those who are emotionally or physically limited in any way. As she mentioned numerous ways to spread her message, I kept thinking, "Does she have any idea how many hours of work and dedication will be required on her part? Will she really be willing to share such private layers of her life?"

~ ~ ~

Mom – Help Me!

Hi Mom,

I am so excited about the prospect of writing this book with Beth but I realize I need your help.

I don't remember some of the details. How sick was I as a baby? Did you wonder why I was sick so often? Were you scared when you first heard the doctor say I had cystic fibrosis?

Looking back and realizing how young you were, I feel badly for you and Daddy. You must have been worried. The only good thing that could have come out of this trauma at such a young age is that it set the tone for what a pain I would be for the next 51 years ... and counting!

So Mom, I am passing the baton to you and asking if you can fill in the missing pieces for me from the beginning. I don't want to bog you down so don't feel like you have to write this history in one day. But in typical Shelly fashion – when can you do this? Soon? Tomorrow? Be honest but don't say too much. Maybe you could reduce the number of times I sneaked out of the house to under 10!

Remember when I was six or seven years old? It was late at night and I had been tucked in bed for hours. I woke up and in a little voice yelled, "Mom, I need a bunny costume for school."

You said, "Okay, Shelly, when do you need it?" I yelled back, "Tomorrow." (Mom, this is the grown-up bunny costume I need!)

Loooooove you,

Shelly

~ ~ ~

Through a Mother's Eyes

Dear Beth,

Obviously you know our daughter, Shelly, has made me aware of every conversation the two of you have had since you first connected. I should begin with a note of appreciation for you and your publisher who believe there's a marketable story about her life. Her father and I, quite naturally, feel everything she does is remarkable – not just her indomitable will but her brain power, her humanity and her inner and outer beauty. There is so much joy associated with being Shelly's mom at her marvelous age of 51 (more like 40). After three children, four grandchildren and now two great grandchildren, let me share what I recall about the day Shelly was born.

The year was 1960. John Kennedy was elected president and Elvis Presley was all the rage. I was two weeks past my due date so I was induced and Shelly was born July 13th. While I loved being pregnant, labor was something else and in those days they didn't do epidurals. You were sedated and introduced to your child (sex unknown until birth) when you awakened. I was at a new hospital, Baptist Memorial Hospital, and Shelly was the first Jewish baby girl born there.

Because there were no ultra sounds performed in those days,

I didn't know until delivery that Shelly was posterior (head down but facing the wrong way). This meant she had to be turned before she could be delivered so no drugs could be given to me as was customary in those days; they needed me to participate. Enough said about this, but it should have been an inkling that Shelly would be contrary later in life and cause me pain although she would bring us great joy as well.

In those years we stayed in the hospital a full five days for girls (Jewish mothers of boys remained in the hospital until the 8th day when the ritual circumcision is performed). Other than a difficult delivery, there was nothing to intimate that she had any kind of illness. Babies remained all together in a glassed-in nursery and visiting hours were very strict; no one as I recall could be in the room when they brought you your baby to nurse or give a bottle and the baby was quickly shunted back to the nursery. When you wanted to view your baby you would put paper on the window with the last name on it and they'd wheel your baby to the front row so everyone could "ohh and ahh" and then another replacement bassinette would be wheeled up.

I was 20 years old when Mindy (our eldest daughter) was born in 1957. She was the perfect infant (slept as long as I wanted her to sleep), the perfect toddler (talked so early) and the perfect older sister to Shelly. My husband, Seymour, was co-owner of a ladies' manufacturing factory in Kansas City and with a partner who was much older, it was Seymour's responsibility to be on the road during the week that sometimes turned into being gone two or three weeks at a time. In those early years his time was primarily focused on the business by necessity. He hated being gone from me and our daughters but he had a business to grow and we had wonderful parents (his and mine) who were of the greatest support.

Shelly was different than our experience with Mindy right from the start. She was sweet, beautiful, tow-haired and mischievous but always sick. Seymour and I were so unsure what to do when she would spike high fevers at a moment's notice so we'd stick her in a bathtub of cool water or rub her down with washcloths drenched in alcohol and water to keep her cool. Her cough was so deep that it rattled. We made a 'tent' for her crib by thumb-tacking a bed sheet over it. Cool air humidifiers were just coming on the scene and we'd struggle with whether the warm air vaporizer or cool air humidifier was better. The tent and sheet on her mattress would get soaked and the fear of making Shelly sicker was always uppermost in our minds.

Our youngest daughter, Lori, was born 15 months after Shelly. Lori had abdominal distresses that took about a year to resolve so she cried a lot and I needed to carry her on my shoulder all day. Our little five-year-old Mindy started her eventual nursing career right from adolescence. She helped me manage "the kids" as she called them. With Seymour out of town, Mindy was my right-hand helper and an expert at folding diapers.

I made numerous emergency trips to the hospital in the middle of the night when Shelly was sick and always dropped Mindy and Lori off at my mother's. I grew weary from all the hospital admissions and receiving no definitive answers to my questions: "What is wrong with Shelly? Why does she have so many bronchial problems and bouts of pneumonia?"

Shelly played hard like all the other kids; in the summer months, however, salt crystals would form on her arms and eyebrows when she'd perspire after running. I remember saying to the doctor, "I know this sounds crazy but she always tastes salty when I kiss her." I was a Mom who cooked healthy foods long before it was fashionable and never used salt in my food preparation or at the table; I preferred using herbs for flavoring. I could never understand why Shelly always asked for salt when we ate. I didn't realize that her body was telling her something we didn't know.

We are an unusually close extended family. Cousins are like brothers and sisters. Thanksgiving dinner means about 38 people with add-ons welcomed. Each year everyone's question is: "Will Shelly be able to come?" As you write her story, you will see three sisters who are each funnier than the other and we all try to be the last one with the best comeback. I feel that's been our saving grace ... love, determination, a good mind and a sense of humor.

With anticipation,

Felicia

~ ~ ~

Through a Father's Eyes

Dear Beth,

I have appreciated the dialogue between you and our family and the trust you and Shelly have developed. You know where the skeletons are hidden and seem to understand with unconditional, nonjudgemental openness how we feel about our lives and each other. As her dad, I can become very emotional just thinking about her.

I have procrastinated contributing information until now; I realize it is because I am more comfortable with my head in the sand than acknowledging the gravity of what Shelly has faced all her life. I marvel that she has done so with such bravery and self-determination. From the first time I learned of her challenge to today, I cannot focus on it without the emotions making me tear up.

Obviously Felicia and I are extremely proud of each of our daughters and grateful for the dynamics of our family, so if this episode focuses on Shelly it doesn't diminish our appreciation and admiration of Mindy and Lori. (We know they know that.) We are each aware that Shelly has lived with a burden the rest of us have not faced. So all the more we recognize how special she is for her accomplishments - and even more for her disposition.

When each of the girls and I look into one another's eyes, we know how we feel about each other and how fortunate we are to be family.

Not enough can be said about Felicia's tremendous effort and influence; her dedication and loving care have bound this family together through all the 'storms.' She often did this solo because my business required me to travel. As a result, Felicia had to wear many hats which she did nobly and admirably. Of course, it bothered me to be gone so much.

The year Mindy was born we started a dress factory business and were minnows in a shark tank of regional and national competition. The early years were a struggle so when the season was weak, it was necessary to travel more to keep up; I didn't dare do less. When the season was more promising, it was time to travel more to take advantage of it. That was the family business for 22 years.

I loved coming home to my beautiful family. After warm hugs from everyone, I would often play a game the girls invented called 'climbing monkeys.' I'd lie on the floor very quietly pretending I was asleep then make scary noises while my three little monkeys climbed all over me. Time spent with them was precious to me and always will be.

An unforgettable event tells how Shelly cares about others more than herself. I returned from a trip one day and pulled up to the garage. I rearranged things on the seat and put the car in reverse to straighten it. At that moment Shelly ran up behind the car to greet me. Thank God I happened to stop just as I saw her in the mirror putting up her hands to ward it off. What was her reaction? She said, "Daddy, if you ever did run me over, don't feel bad 'cause I would know you didn't mean to." Tears come to my eyes right now as I think about that day. That was Shelly then and that is Shelly now.

She is so charismatic! Everyone who meets her considers her their best friend - both men and women. She has a special ability for reading and understanding people and is the spark plug for everything going on around her. Instead of being depressed which would be so understandable, she is always inspiringly up and ambitious. She doesn't see a cloud hanging over her; she looks ahead to the sunshine. She knows she is always in our prayers and we in hers.

In closing, I wish to thank you for your interest in our Shelly and your open, comfortable format for this dialogue.

Sincerely,

Seymour

~ ~ ~

The Disease

Dear Beth,

During one of Shelly's hospitalizations when she was nine years old, I really felt a better answer was needed other than "she has bronchitis and some pneumonia." I discharged our pediatrician late one evening (a difficult thing to do because he had become a friend), and went to the nurse's station and engaged a pediatrician I knew many of my friends used. When he asked if Shelly had ever been given a sweat test, I said that she hadn't and that I wasn't familiar with it. He said the test was an indicator for cystic fibrosis but wanted to test her first before going further into it. I didn't know he was head of the Cystic Fibrosis Clinic at the University of Kansas Medical Center.

Shelly's tests were inconclusive: once positive and once negative. This 'borderline CF' confused us even more. What did this mean exactly? The doctor also explained that she didn't fit the usual parameters of a cystic fibrosis patient at this age which included issues with pancreatic function, a failure to thrive and a very thin body structure. This wasn't Shelly. She ate well and was chubby. Because of her history, he put her on the cystic fibrosis regimen of daily inhalation therapy, postural drainage and clapping therapy to clear her lungs and vigorous oral antibiotics when needed.

Seymour and I were stunned to learn that CF was genetic and that in order to have this disease, we both had to be carriers of the defective CF gene. In sheer disbelief, we asked why our other two daughters were spared. The doctor explained there was a 25% chance that each of the girls could have been born with CF and a 25% chance they would not. As the statistics swirled through our minds, fear became agony when we asked about Shelly's prognosis.

We would be forever haunted by those eight paralyzing words: "Your daughter will have a shortened life span." We were told that children with the disease usually didn't survive beyond the age of six years old. Shelly was already beyond that and given that her overall health (outside of lung congestion) was good, we couldn't believe or accept the harsh reality of the diagnosis. As we left the office holding Shelly's hands, Seymour and I were determined to provide her with a normal life as much as possible; we were determined not to dwell on the dire statistics of her disease.

When I discovered that Hahnemann Medical Center in Philadelphia was the leading center in the treatment of cystic fibrosis, I asked Dr. Kanarek to make an introduction for us and send the necessary papers for Shelly to be seen there. She was 12 at that time and even though she resisted all efforts of therapy, it was time for some definitive answers.

Felicia

~ ~ ~

In the Dark of Night

When our children are born we discover something new within us, a depth of love that can't be verbalized. This new awareness is something God tucks away in our souls just waiting to be found…just waiting for that miraculous moment when we hold our newborns and feel the beating of their hearts in perfect rhythm with our own.

We know God has entrusted us with gifts whom we will nurture with love and care. We do the very best we can to keep them safe and shield them from the painful barbs of reality. We give them solid roots in order to grow and sturdy wings in order to soar.

Our job is to hug our children with pride and comfort them when they fall; we are the ones to whom they will turn when they're confused and in search of their identities. They know we will be there to bandage their scraped knees and provide unconditional support for decisions made wisely and unwisely.

Felicia and Seymour were entrusted with the safekeeping of three gifts of life. They had no way of knowing that one of these gifts would come into the world with unhealthy lungs that would never heal. They grieved in silence knowing they couldn't rescue their daughter from every storm that lay ahead. As they prayed in the dark of night, helpless tears fell on their pillows. They grieved in knowing they could never hold her in their arms and promise her that she would soon feel better. They grieved that they had unwittingly passed on a genetic disease that would rob Shelly of the same healthy life her two sisters would have.

~ ~ ~

No Way!

It really didn't mean anything to Shelly when she first heard the words 'cystic fibrosis.' She already knew she didn't feel well much of the time; she just wanted some medicine to make things better. The word 'disease' sounded like a real burden and a life-long illness to her.

That was probably the day she started hating the word 'sick.' She loathed that word so much that she would abruptly correct anyone in her family who used the word to describe how she was feeling. Having a cold or the flu usually lasted a week but being sick sounded like a lifetime sentence, something she did not want – ever.

She remembered testing positive on her first sweat test and negative on the second one. She really wasn't too concerned because she was sure all along that whatever she had was not what the doctors thought. At that point Felicia decided they needed some answers once and for all, so she sought the premiere medical center in the country that treated teenagers who had cystic fibrosis.

Shelly was excited about the trip that lay ahead; she was 12 years old and still at the age where she loved being with her mom – just the two of them. She was looking forward to visiting the Franklin Mint, the White House, Bookbinders for seafood and then spend just a day or two at the Hahnemann Medical Center which she had completely blocked out of her mind.

She clearly remembered the day she met her doctor and not feeling afraid because he was a kind, caring man with a wonderful sense of humor that put her at ease. She didn't complain when he wanted her to have another sweat test because at that time this was the only way to diagnose CF. She rationalized that the sooner the tests were over the sooner she and her mother could have fun on this vacation she envisioned.

To be tested, she had to dress in very warm clothes while nurses attached sticky patches to her skin which were actually electrodes that would stimulate her sweat glands. Then she was asked to exercise as much as possible so they could determine how much sweat she lost from perspiring. Even at a young age she felt like this was such an unsophisticated way to make a diagnosis, especially in an old dark brick building that was sterile and uninviting. But she did what she was told and repeatedly walked up and down the stairway of steps and paced the different floors of the hospital until she started to sweat.

Shortly afterwards the doctor came into the treatment room and said it was a positive diagnosis. Shelly definitely had cystic fibrosis. Felicia could not contain her tears while Shelly viewed everything as an inconvenience. Her biggest fear was that her mother was going to make her be a sick person now, that she would try to slow her down and not let her do all the things her friends were doing.

~ ~ ~

How Stupid!

Shelly paid absolutely no attention to the doctor as he spent a great deal of time talking about her disease and the treatments that would be required. It simply sounded boring. The only two things she remembered were his teaching her how to cough without hurting herself and describing how she could expect to feel as she got older. He prefaced the 'older' part by saying that she could live well into her teens and maybe live to be 13 or even 18 years old. In Shelly's mind he said it with such a false sense of happiness - as if it were encouraging news. In her mind he was talking about a 'different' Shelly because she had no intentions of dying at such a young age.

He went into detail explaining why it was important with CF to always clear her lungs with a productive cough or otherwise the secretions would sit in the lung cavities creating bacteria which would promote her disease. He warned that her coughing could be very violent at times and to be sure she anchored herself to prevent pulling a muscle. Once again she thought, "Boring. I'm not putting that much thought into a cough." The doctor did catch her attention, however, when he said, "Eventually you will have bouts of coughing up blood which will become frequent with the progression of your disease."

None of this was real. Why did he think he could put her mind at ease about coughing up blood when she only had the chance to live to her teenage years? Why was he even telling her this? Why was her mom holding her hand and rubbing it? Why had her mother even brought her here? It was stupid and she would not be someone who was sick. Ever!

The doctor then explained her required daily treatments which included continuing to use her nebulizer to deliver breathing treatments that were increased to three times a day. He also demonstrated how Felicia and Seymour were to perform postural drainage and percussion treatments twice a day to help break up the congestion sitting in her lungs. He showed Shelly how to lie with her head lower than her feet on an incline while her parents cupped their hands and percussed her sides, lower lungs, upper lungs and shoulders. She thought to herself, "Why is he even wasting his breath? I'm not going to do this. It's too weird. I don't want Mom and Dad to spend hours a day hitting me like that. I don't have time for this. I don't have time to do the stupid breathing treatments either. I want to run and play and go to a friend's house after school and watch TV late at night."

Shelly subconsciously said to herself, "Look out, Mom and Dad, you are in for a real treat trying to slow me down. If you try, I promise to make your lives miserable every time you attempt to get me to take care of myself."

Her strategy was to go on the defense so she started thinking of creative and defiant ways to avoid this CF business. She promised herself that she wouldn't give in and wouldn't be sick. End of story.

The emotional day concluded with the doctor telling them about a great group of CF patients they had at the medical center and what a strong support system they were for one another. He asked Shelly if she would like to come back the following day and join them. She had absolutely no interest in meeting sick people with a disease she couldn't relate to at all. They were sick and she was not. Felicia said they would come back some other time.

This was the best news Shelly heard all day. Finally she and her mother were going to go sight-seeing and have fun. Finally they were going to follow Shelly's plan from the start.

~ ~ ~

Through a Sister's Eyes

Dear Beth,

This is Mindy. You'll have to forgive our family for the many emails being exchanged which have become a love-fest for us as we recall and share the various stages of our lives and our pure admiration for my sister, Shelly (Shell).

We had a great childhood. Even though Shell's illness must have been the first and last thing on our parents' minds, Lori and I never felt overshadowed. Shelly is the most fun, caring, bright, ambitious and beautiful person I know – physically and emotionally. If she ever felt bitter that she had a disease, I don't recall it. In fact, I don't recall her ever 'playing the CF card.'

What I do recall is her always 'getting' to be in the mist tent. (Once she and Lori got to share one and I was a bit jealous.) The wet sheets in the tent always seemed like they'd be cold so I decided it didn't look that fun and the novelty wore off. I knew Mom (my parenting partner) had a lot more work to do when we had to take care of Shell in the tent.

I was in high school when we were still going on the borderline CF test result premise. I read about all the truly sick kids with CF and knew enough about probability to think there are 'false positive' test results. I forever thought the doctors would soon be able to prove Shell just had a coughing problem –certainly not CF.

I'm embarrassed now as an adult that I was jealous as a teenager when Mom and Shell got to have a special trip to Philadelphia even though I knew the purpose. What I thought was going to be a vacation for them didn't turn out that way. I thought they'd return home with good news. This was not the case. I remember Dad being sad and teary when he explained that Mom had called and said Shell's test results at Hahnemann were not good.

When they returned home, Mom did sit us down and said, "You can't catch it" and "Shell won't make your friends sick," and there were some new therapies she would need. There was also a more private, unnerving talk about life expectancy. Since that time I have built a magical brick wall that I hide behind to avoid ever believing Shell has 'that kind of CF.' (I think I've always believed in my heart and mind – even though I know intellectually it's not true – that maybe she really has a mild form of CF since she doesn't have the pancreatic issues many CF people do.)

There were times when I felt my parents chose to excuse some of her poor decisions (boyfriends, behavior, etc.) because they felt some guilt about her having this terrible disease. As a sister in a bit of denial that Shell who was so vibrant had anything to worry about, I felt like she should have been reigned in more. Easy for me to say now when I look back. As a parent and grandparent, I realize the much bigger things I have excused in my own life and my children's lives.

We all remember Mom sitting us down with a cigarette and handkerchief. She had us take a drag and then blow the smoke through the handkerchief to see the grey residue it left behind. I was embarrassed at times by her necessary but forceful messages to anyone who dared come into our house smelling like smoke. To this day she has trouble hiding her disrespect for a smoker knowing what she would give for her daughter to have healthy lungs versus someone opting to damage theirs.

Shell was the entrepreneur in our family. During our break from Hebrew school she would walk through our neighborhood selling the icons of the late 60's and 70's that included cinnamon toothpicks and those hanging banging balls called clackers. Mom was active in religious, philanthropic and community endeavors that also involved fund-raisers. Shell sold whatever Mom needed to sell whether it was bric-a-brac, purse calendars or key chains. She was a natural. I admired that about her. Truthfully I admired everything about her and always will.

Wishing Shelly's book great success,

Mindy

~ ~ ~

Through Another Sister's Eyes

Dear Beth,

Shelly is and always has been my hero. So is my oldest sister Mindy. Mindy and I are four years apart in age and Shelly and I often believed she was too mature and had no interest in playing with us. Shelly and I are only 15 months apart in age so we were natural playmates.

We played together as kids, were close during our pre-teen and teenage years and then as young adults before she permanently moved out of town. As a young child I called her "Eddie" and no one else was allowed to call her that. That was my special name for her and as I recall, she was protective of that. Shelly always included me. I was not aware of it if she was bothered by her little sister tagging along.

There were times though when she would threaten me with "If you tell Mom I'm gonna kill you" or something along those lines. These were, of course, the times she coaxed me into doing things that we had no business doing. Shelly had a way of conniving (recurring theme here) people either to pay for things they may not realize they needed or she convinced them to give her things she thought she needed more than they did. She would charge me, her little sister, a quarter to let me buckle her dress that was just hanging in her closet!

Growing up I had no idea that Shelly had a disease, let alone a serious one. Looking back I can't believe I lived in the same house and could be so oblivious to her illness. I remember her coughing so much and having a lot of phlegm. We'd say, "Stop snicking" and she'd say, "I can't help it." That was about the extent of it. I don't remember her saying she couldn't breathe or needing to clear her throat. Maybe she was being protective of me?

When we did have the family talk, the story about Shelly having borderline CF seemed to have stuck with me also. I truly believed this because she has always been so vibrant, full of energy and 'everything to everybody.' She has never been a complainer; instead she asks about everyone else and their problems or ailments. She always deflects attention from herself.

The first time I remember ever hearing about the seriousness of Shelly's CF was when I read a feature article about her in a St. Louis magazine that described her unyielding determination and phenomenal professional success. It stated that Shelly's original diagnosed life expectancy was 18 and I couldn't believe my eyes. She was probably 35 years old at the time. I was, of course, upset with my family for never telling me this. I was also upset with myself that I could let Shelly go through this alone without me; I was in shock. I guess my parents really did have the foresight not to allow this diagnosis to rule her life or ours.

As grown-ups we three sisters still laugh about so many wonderful childhood memories. We really had a great neighborhood and friends and that is what seems to stick out in our minds. Although we live in three different cities, it is a rarity if more than a day or two goes by without talking on the phone to one another or to Mom and Dad.

Wishing you well in telling our heroic sister's life,

Lori

~ ~ ~

The Sisterhood

It's funny, Beth, but I don't know if my sisters and I ever discussed my trip to Philadelphia. I don't think they ever really asked about what the doctor said and I don't know that I ever mentioned it. I'm sure they knew I was diagnosed with CF but it didn't really mean a great deal to me at the time so I'm sure it meant even less to them. If I had to guess I would say I probably didn't want to make a big deal about it. I didn't want anyone feeling sorry for me and I didn't want to feel sorry for myself. I do remember always saying, "You don't know what it's like. I can't breathe." I remember feeling like I was suffocating.

I am certain if you ask my sisters about growing up with me and CF, they really won't have too many memories of my being affected by it. It's only been in the last five years that they have seen the negative impact it has had on my health. Yes, my sisters would probably say they have more memories of me being a troublemaker, a rebel and always doing something that was just flat out wrong. That was the case but in my defense I think I looked worse because my sisters were so good!

Lori (LorLor) was sweet, quiet and innocent. She always used to say, "No one ever listens to me." I can hear her saying that now. She was always so good in school and never caused problems. She was smart and had lots of friends. Mindy (Min) was mature, intelligent, reliable and hid anything she did wrong so well that Mom and Dad knew she was a saint.

When you have two sisters it is important to learn the art of intimidation in order to survive. When you are fighting for phone time, bathroom time, favorite foods and privacy, you are forced to be creative and evil. I think I really had that perfected with LorLor. I had her under my little sister spell.

She was gullible and wanted to hang out with her older sister. I loved it because she was so much fun, made me laugh and could keep a secret. That was the deal- you can hang out but if you tell Mom and Dad anything - you are out. I don't want to paint this picture like I was a horrible sister to Lori because I did a lot for her. For instance, I had a dress that she loved because it had really cool buckles. So we made a deal. If she would secretly make my bed every morning I would 'let' her go in my closet and buckle my dress. Or if we were playing outside and I got hungry, I would 'let' her run home and get me a snack and still 'let' her be the one who couldn't find us in hide-and-go-seek. It was the perfect win-win. As much as I tortured LorLor, she is my little sister whom I love more than life; I would do anything in the world for her.

Mindy was not so easy to manipulate because she had one thing over us- credibility! Mom and Dad believed and trusted her and she was responsible for us. The good news is that she had to serve us and keep us happy when she baby-sat. Oh boy, did Lori and I torture her! We were a tag team. Mindy was smart and I still am not sure to this day if she locked herself in her room to study every day just to avoid Lori and me or if she was motivated to study by her fear of getting a 'B' in school - heaven forbid.

I know Mindy remembers my having bronchitis or pneumonia often because unfortunately she was on 'filling the humidifier' duty. Lori and I found great joy in playing this game at Min's expense. Back then humidifiers were about 4 feet in circumference and there was a big open cavity you had to fill with water. Of course the sinks were not nearly big enough to accommodate that size so you had to bend over and lower it into a bathtub. By the time it was filled it weighed close to 20 pounds (I may be exaggerating) and then she had to lift it back out of the tub. Then she had to balance the water and walk it down the hall to my room without spilling it.

That was a feat in itself. Lori and I thought it would be fun to make this even a bit more challenging for Mindy so we would hide … and wait… and as soon as she took her first steps down the hall with this sloshing open cavity of water we would yell "NICOBAN!" which was our secret word for all-out war on Mindy.

Each of us would grab one of her legs, pull them apart and lift them off the ground. (I wonder if that is why she broke her pelvic bone later in life?) Then as half the water supply would spill on the high-pile shag carpeting, we would take off leaving her to clean up everything and start the whole process over again.

Poor Min. She was voted 'the most humorous' in high school and Lori and I tested her sense of humor daily while she took care of us when Mom and Dad were working. It's no surprise that she graduated at the top of her class and went on to be a nurse and take care of others. Everyone loves and relies on Mindy.

My two sisters are my best friends. The three of us always had so much fun and whether it was Saturday tap dance, jazz and ballet lessons, swimming lessons or long trips in the back of a station wagon each summer, we had the best childhood any sisters could have.

The only part about growing up I don't like is living so far away from each other. However, that is also the best thing about having your sisters as your best friends; they are there no matter what.

~ ~ ~

An Afternoon with Felicia

Dear Felicia,

There are so many things I'd like to ask you that it's difficult knowing where to begin. I, too, am a mother and know those feelings of desperation when we can't mend our children's pain. We are forever the caregivers, aren't we? When our children's hearts ache, ours ache even more.

Let's imagine that we're sharing a cup of coffee in friendship and I ask, "Felicia, how were you able to remain so strong when Shelly was diagnosed with a disease that little was known about at the time? Where did you turn for help? Where did you find refuge when your worries were too heavy to bear? How were you able to handle or justify Shelly's defiant behavior?

Let's imagine that we're spending the entire afternoon together. I'll listen while you tell me everything you can about Shelly, her disease, how it affected you and how it affected the family.

With appreciation,
Beth

Dear Beth:

In responding to your email, many things stand out. Let me ramble on and begin by saying our kids were a ball of fun; they were loving, funny, and imaginative in making up plays, recitals, parades, etc. Shelly always wanted to try any new adventure and was an eager participant in gymnastics, dance classes and softball teams. Unless she was really sick, she never opted out of participating in any activity because she didn't feel well.

When Shell was in middle school, she was the catcher on the local YMCA girls' softball team. Their coach must have been, I think, a retired Marine drill sergeant as he would run them around the field for any slight mistake and in Midwest summers, the heat and humidity can be brutal. I used to give her salt pills before these activities and I really wanted her to quit the team. She refused and since it gave her some good clearing coughing when she got home, I agreed to let her continue. At one point,

Shelly had done something to one of her knees and was on crutches; her team was playing for the league championship and she was the catcher. There was no stopping her. She walked to the field on crutches and played, down on one knee in a catcher's stance. Isn't it funny? I can't remember if they won or lost; what mattered is that Shelly had persevered, never letting herself or her team down.

I wrote a lot of skits, parodies and put on plays or other programs for many philanthropic organizations. When appropriate the girls would go with me for rehearsals, often doing their own. They participated alongside us working for those less fortunate. I would see their tender, caring hearts and listen to their questions afterwards that were beyond their years. Shell always worried about people being cold.

I think because of my young age at parenthood and with Seymour working so much, I involved them in a lot of my days. However, the girls had boundaries and they knew them well. A look sometimes was all that was necessary and the message got across. Shelly did like to push the edge but nothing more than any child who is strong-willed and doesn't give up the first time or second or third or ever. As I look back now, in the long run this may have been one of her saving qualities. What may have tried our patience then, may have been the beginning signs of the strong will she would need later in her life.

Shell was not rebellious as a child or even later which might sound strange but I'll explain as I go. She did everything with reckless abandon and had such charm about her that you wanted to be with her. Even though she was often made fun of in grade school and middle school because of her weight, she never lacked for friends and wasn't excluded from any "invites."

We spent a lot of time with family and vacationed every summer with my sister and her family. Because everyone spent so much time with Shell in all types of settings and activities, we were always questioned about her cough, the clearing of her throat, etc. They knew well how many times I ran her to the hospital in the middle of the night, about all the doctors' visits and the medicines she took. So little was known about CF in the

60's and everything I learned I had to research at the various medical center libraries. Seymour and I searched desperately to find pulmonary specialists in the country who were experts in diagnosing and treating her disease.

Then everything began to change after Shelly and I made our first trip to Hahnemann Medical Center when she was 12. We immediately liked her doctor's disposition and his team.

While Shelly was meeting privately with the social worker to discuss her fears, etc., the doctor told me what to expect and not just medically. He explained that when children grow up with a disease from infancy they get used to a regimen, a way of life and of "being different."

When Dr. Holsclaw was explaining what the positive diagnosis for Shelly of cystic fibrosis meant, the aggressive treatments required to help slow down the eventual deterioration of her lung functions, I heard no other words. This couldn't be happening to my child - - to us. We were a happy, laughing family. Sure, we had problems like everyone else dealing with life, but this? Immediately I thought how would I explain this to her sisters? Seymour would think we should protect them completely and tell them nothing really dire. But I knew that they couldn't be left in the dark. Mindy at 15 was bright enough to search out information on her own. Lori (not yet 11) was Shell's playmate; what do you say to her? Would this change our family dynamics forever? I was 32 years old. How do I deal with this future for my child? To be honest, I probably utilized the same denial that Shelly inherited. I'll play by their rules, but I know we'll be able to overcome this. I won't let it happen; not to my child.

He said that Shelly's age was the worst for a diagnosis like this, that it was a time in her life when kids are just going into their teens and want to be like all their peers. He said this would be a difficult pill for her to swallow. He told me to anticipate behavior problems, disobedience and things we could never guess she'd be capable of doing. He explained that it would be a tough road ahead for us. Knowing how Shelly always felt about being referred to as sick, I worried but knew my basically loving, basically caring child would never put me through all these things.

Little did I know or didn't know.

How did we tolerate this behavior? Why were there no bars put on her? Of course she suffered consequences when she broke the rules; of course we had restrictions for her as well as her two sisters; of course every infraction was a test of wills. Beth, you questioned how Shelly can get through an entire hour of live TV on HSN without coughing or clearing her throat. That is the same will she exhibited in denying her disease, fighting any verbalized outcome and any behavior that she knew was risky but never considered really dangerous. As involved, aware and savvy as Seymour and I were as parents, Shelly was able to pull the wool over our eyes many times - for the moment. We usually found out the truth by either outsmarting her or recognizing the inconsistencies in her answers. We were torn in how to proceed. Should her punishments be any greater than those we'd impose on the other girls if they exhibited that behavior? Did we excuse some because of being pre-warned to expect it? Could we put ourselves in her place if we were given the same death sentence at her age? What were we to do? Crying a lot helped but being of that same strong-willed nature that Shelly inherited, I never asked anyone for help. Today I would; I would seek counseling. You just didn't in those days.

This may sound unbelievable but during all of this I had a basic trust in Shelly. I knew that she was making some really bad decisions, but I felt deep down that it would all settle itself out. I just knew that she had growing pains associated with the natural maturation process. Sometimes, I must admit, it caused a real serious difference of opinion between Seymour and me. I think he felt I really needed to reign her in more. Easy to say. I knew he was right but I just had to let this work itself out and although some really stupid decisions were made on her part, she was still that good girl who was trying to grow up too fast. Was it because she thought she wouldn't? If she had only known that I said if anything was going to kill her it would be me, not a disease!

Fondly,

Felicia

~ ~ ~

Painfully Different

Shelly only had one friend in school who knew she had CF. She felt safe telling her because this girl suffered from diabetes. They were somewhat of a codependent pair and were both in denial of their diseases.

Other than this school friend, no one knew about the secret Shelly harbored day after day. She already felt painfully different from everyone else at school and didn't need to add CF to the mix. She was Jewish and there were only two other Jewish kids in her class; one classmate wouldn't admit it because there was still visible prejudice in the schools at the time.

Then there was the burden of being overweight for her age. As if her school days weren't filled with enough physical and emotional torment, Shelly's gymnastics teacher referred to her as "the skinny kid with the big bones." Though embarrassed by the hurtful words, it wasn't as demeaning as the name she was called by the popular jocks. She never forgot the pain of their cruel mockery that echoed down the hall when they yelled, "Hey, tush hog."

~ ~ ~

Denial

Shelly, I sense there is more for you to share in terms of your friendship with the girl who had diabetes. Did you remain friends throughout school? What role did you play in the friendship? Were you the caregiver? Open up these feelings that are hidden from view.

Beth

~ ~ ~

Mixed Emotions

This is hard to talk about Beth. I guess I've blocked it out of my mind purposely. Growing up with a disease is tough enough but being at an age where you want to fit in and not be judged is even harder. Kids can be cruel.

Disguising the fact that I had a genetic disease was imperative and it was important that no one ever knew. I did not want to be judged as different. Therefore, only two friends of mine even knew I had a disease. My friend with diabetes had her own struggles in life so it was an easy choice for me to let her into my secret world. She was already ostracized by others for having her own affliction and the more she shared with others, the more the kids shut her out. While I could somewhat relate to her internal pain, I could never understand why she let others know of her illness.

We were polarizing opposites in how we dealt with our challenges but there was one thing we had in common; we made perfect co-dependents. She had a very good understanding of her disease and how it should be managed in order to stay healthy and alive. She understood it so well that she was in control of mismanaging it to her own benefit. She used her insulin and blood sugar level monitoring as a tool to manage her physical image. She was a binge eater, put her body into nearly a state of insulin shock and then cheated with her insulin shot levels so she would remain thin. She was more consumed with the way she looked physically than how long she would live. Her goal was to remain thin and attractive at all costs.

I, on the other hand, was in complete denial of my disease. I didn't care about taking care of myself and had no interest in learning anything about it. I wanted to ignore it and push the limits as far as I could just to prove I was not sick. We were a perfect pair in one respect; we both had a motivation for abusing our health and sabotaging our own lives. We were also a dangerous pair and pushed the limits in every possible way.

She was angry at the world and hated the fact she had been

cursed with diabetes. I felt very sorry for her because she had something she had to cope with day in and day out whereas I didn't really deal with my CF. I didn't think of myself as being in her category. She was very bitter and this led her down the path of depression and guilt on a daily basis. Because I was the only one who was close to her and knew the specifics of her disease, I was the daily sounding board and counselor. I spent countless hours listening to her problems and trying to find a way to make her feel better. Her problems and worries became mine and it was up to me to try to help cheer her up. The more she complained, the more she alienated herself from other friends she had along the way. She was somewhat of a downer for everyone and I was the one who wanted to help if I could.

Over time this pattern of behavior began to wear on me; I could see the quality of her life diminishing and she wouldn't assume any responsibility in changing it. By the end of high school I became more intolerant of her self-destructive attitude. I realized that no matter how hard I tried, she did not want help.

One weekend she called me and left a few messages that she needed to talk. I was so busy and working that I planned to call her back in a few days to see what she needed and how I could help. I never got that chance. I received a call that she had taken her own life. She had asked her mother to come stay at her new apartment with her and while her mom was in the TV room, she ended her life in her bedroom. I had such mixed emotions when I heard the news. I was disappointed and angry that she couldn't find a way to enhance her life. How could anyone just give up?

I was angry that she didn't care about everyone else in her life who cared about her. How could someone be so selfish not to live for others who need you? I had my own issues to deal with but I could never imagine inflicting so much hurt and pain on someone else, just to make my life "easier" or to relieve my own pain. How could she do that to her mom? How could she do that to her family? How could she do that to me?

Because of my disease, I always look at others' afflictions in life and say "Could I do it? Could I live that life?" I realize the answer always has to be "yes" and the real secret is finding a way to make "YES" mean something. You have to find a way to celebrate small victories. Don't just live for today. Embrace tomorrow and make it happen.

~ ~ ~

The Brave Underdog

As if living with CF weren't enough of a prison sentence, Shelly's body and self-esteem were handcuffed further in elementary school. She struggled to focus and pay attention because she couldn't breathe comfortably half the time, could not stop coughing, spit up phlegm and had a runny nose. She tried so hard not to cough and disturb the class but the more she tried to repress it, the louder and harder she coughed.

Some of her teachers were very understanding and allowed her to go to the bathroom where she could cough privately; some were also very understanding in helping her catch up with her homework when she missed numerous days of school. When one of her favorite teachers announced to the class that she had to take a leave of absence, Shelly panicked in fear of having a substitute teacher who wouldn't understand her situation. To alleviate her fears, Felicia wrote a letter for Shelly to give to this person that said: "Please allow Shelly to be excused to go to the bathroom whenever needed."

After Shelly discreetly handed the letter to the substitute teacher, she returned to her desk as quickly as possible. The lady followed her, opened the letter in front of everyone and as she read it took her pointer finger and hit the top of Shelly's shoulder with every word she uttered. In a staccato voice that mimicked the tone of the letter, she pounded on Shelly's shoulder and read:

"Please allow Shelly to go to the bathroom whenever needed." If this emotional abuse weren't enough, she caustically added, "Well, Miss Shelly, what makes you so special that you think you can disrupt class and leave when you want?"

Shelly was speechless and totally mortified. She wanted to fall through the floor and die right there. Instead she asked for permission to go to the nurse's office, a place where she spent a great deal of time in primary school because she was usually sick. This particular day, however, she sought refuge where she could call her mother or Grammy to come rescue her from the unconscionable torment she had just endured.

But Shelly's revenge came a few days later when the substitute teacher was in the bathroom at the same time Shelly was. As she came out to the sink area she was zipping up her skirt. Her half slip got caught as she zipped up her zipper, but her slip hung out the top and draped down like a long white tail. Shelly started to say something, thinking she could get on her good side. Then she came to her senses and realized how much more fun it would be to let her walk out into the classroom with a tail. So she said nothing and just smiled politely as they left the bathroom.

~ ~ ~

A Hero Steps Forward

"Hi Shelly. It's Beth. How are feeling today?"

"I feel great, Partner. I had a good run this morning. That's a relief because the past two days have been harder for me. I still ran my three miles but it feels like my left lung is missing some air. Ironically, my right lung almost always hurts but my left is worse now."

"When is your next appointment with the doctor?"

"In a few weeks but I'm not worried about it. Let's change the subject and talk about the book. You're probably going to need new information from me, aren't you?"

"In a few days or so but today I just want to talk. Is this a good time? Have you finished all your breathing treatments?"

"I'm good. This is a perfect time to talk. Fire away and I'll try to answer."

"I only have a few questions but you can't avoid them by changing the subject."

"I was afraid of that. You've already picked up on my tricks. When did you figure this out?"

"It didn't take long, my friend. So here we go and be totally honest. No more games of playing hide-and-seek. Agreed?"

"Agreed. I'll tell the truth but go easy on me."

"It took so much courage to go to school each day and live in your secret world of denial. I can't imagine how you endured the embarrassment of being chastised for your weight. You would have never mocked or taunted a classmate, would you?"

"No. If anything, I was always trying to help someone else through a tough time. I've never been one to hold grudges or be bitter. That might sound corny but it's the truth."

"Can you remember a time in elementary school when you made a conscious effort to help someone when your other classmates didn't?"

"That's easy. When I was in 1st grade, I had a crush on a boy in my class. His name was George. He was cute and had a slight build. He had a large curve in his back which made him look "funny" to everyone, especially when he walked. We didn't understand that he had muscular dystrophy which would take his life at a young age."

"Do you think you empathized with the pain he was feeling as an underdog because it was the same pain you endured?"

"Probably. I do know it made me really mad when kids made fun of him. By second grade, he had even more trouble walking and keeping his balance. Our teacher asked for a volunteer who would be George's helper and physically lift him up. She needed someone to stand by him at recess and steady his balance so a strong wind couldn't knock him to the ground. She asked if any of us would be willing to help carry his lunch tray and be "George's helper" for the school year. I didn't hesitate for a moment and said, "I'll help George."

"Was this a prelude to more events in your life when you thought you could always save or help others?"

"It was a big-time prelude to some very self-destructive things I did in my later years. I put myself in vulnerable positions because I really thought I could change people's lives for the better. You have no idea what lies ahead in my book where I make one serious mistake after another in my relationships with men. You'll be shocked by my bad judgment. Believe me!"

~ ~ ~

The Young Entrepreneur and the Accomplished Liar

The only part of elementary school Shelly enjoyed was time spent helping George survive the day. Her mantra became: "School is a waste of time!" Yet she loved learning outside the formal classroom. She reveled in experimenting with things like shampoo and mouthwash which she brewed until they turned to mold. Many of her concoctions resulted in the house smelling awful for days. This budding chemist was always thinking, "I wonder what would happen if I … "

Shelly's unrelenting curiosity and her passion for selling were formulas for success. These childhood experiments were harbingers of great things to come. This young entrepreneur was on her way to fame and didn't know it.

Shelly was also on her way to self-destruction and did know it. She just didn't care. She fought doing her breathing treatments and refused to acknowledge the lethal consequences of her disease. Instead she became an accomplished liar. When her mother repeatedly reminded her to do the treatments, she retreated to the bathroom, her private den of deception. This is where she turned on the loud therapy machine that she didn't use and waited the mandatory number of minutes the treatment should have taken. Once she turned it off, she waited for her mother to call out, "Shelly, are you done with your treatments?"

With no hesitation or remorse, she routinely replied, "Yeah, Mom, I'm done."

~ ~ ~

The Girls in the Hood

Dear Shelly,

I know you're nervous about sharing bits and pieces from your rebellious past that you want to forget. You're afraid of sending the wrong message to those teenagers and adults whose lives you desperately want to touch in positive ways. You're doing a good job of hiding some regrettable moments behind your sparkling sense of humor. Yet you know that you need to tell your story completely.

You need to find a comfortable but candid starting point. Ironically I received a delightful email today from your high school friend, Lori G. who has shared some of your humorous, mischievous and fearless experiences as teenagers. You've now found your starting point with her email that begins: I've known Shelly since we were five years old and neighbors in Bridlespur. She has always been the natural center of attention with her witty humor, beauty and blonde hair which was unique among the dark-haired Jewish girls 'in the hood.'

From Lori G.

The Weiner home was also the center of attention. We spent the majority of our time together there. As we grew into our teen years the activity generally took off from there.

Our parents belonged to conservative synagogues that were more religious than most in Kansas City. We attended Hebrew school three times per week and didn't really care about any of it. As part of our religious schooling, we were members of the local youth group. The organization had a religious theme and we traveled to Omaha and Des Moines for winter and spring conventions. We also attended a very religious Jewish summer camp in Wisconsin. The irony is that we Bridlespur girls were named "The Unholy 6." We ditched most of the programs and services to hang out and party!

Felicia's 1967 Pontiac Bonneville, which was now Mindy's car, served as

Shelly's practice driving car way before she was 16. She treated us to joy rides around Kansas City including one memorable shopping trip far from home to the Westin Crown Center. The parking garage was a challenge for petite Shelly and that wide Bonneville didn't make the turns up the parking garage too easily. The concrete pillars were unforgiving on the car as she hit the front bumper, reversed and hit the back bumper.

She once got caught driving illegally by one of our older male friends who was so in love with her. He would do anything for her including letting all of us drive his car while underage. For some reason he felt the need to run a movie camera when Shelly was behind the wheel of the Bonneville and show it to Mr. and Mrs. Weiner! This friend wasn't the only guy who liked her. All the neighbor boys did. We played a lot of 'spin the bottle' and 'seven minutes in heaven' in the Weiner basement.

One night after our curfew we invited a couple of the neighbor boys to sneak up to Shelly's room. The problem was we couldn't get them out. Her room was directly across from the bathroom and Mindy had gotten extremely ill that night. Felicia stayed up with her all night long. The boys spent the entire night in Shelly's very full, walk-in closet complaining that there were too many shoes to sit comfortably.

This is Lori G's version of the story, Shelly. What say you, Leader of the Pack?

Beth

~ ~ ~

Shelly's Version of the Story

Well, Beth, my friend Lori G. and I have slightly different recollections of the night my friends were stuffed in my closet. Let me tell you what I told Mom. I have to blame Mindy for everything that happened that night. Our plan would have worked to perfection if she hadn't gotten sick in the middle of the night while staying at a friend's house. This meant Mom and

Dad had to go get her. (The original plan was to sneak out of the house at 1 a.m. to meet the boys.) While my parents were gone, it only seemed like the polite thing to do and invite them in which I did.

We were all hanging out in the kitchen when I heard the garage door open suddenly. I had misjudged how soon Mom and Dad would be back and didn't have time to let our friends out the front door without being seen. So I did the next logical thing. I told the boys to run upstairs and hide in my closet. I figured that Mom would take Mindy upstairs to bed and she'd be asleep in minutes. Then everyone could sneak back out of the house. This was a good plan but bad execution.

Mindy was sick all night and Mom was right there by her side. I finally grew concerned about my friends being stuffed in my closet with no air. I gave up by 7 a.m. and told my hostages to return to their homes and face the music. I marched five people down through the kitchen while Mom and Dad sat at the kitchen table in shock.

Sneaking out of the house became a part-time job for me. I never got it to the point of perfection even though I did it probably 10 times or more. In retrospect I know it was stupid and dangerous. At my age now I am afraid to walk through my house alone with the lights off so the thought of sneaking out just floors me. I feel badly that I dragged my little sister into that mess but it was worth the laughs it has brought us all. Right Mom?

~ ~ ~

What Was I Thinking?

Hi Beth,

I was just reading some of my old diary entries dating back to 1976 when I was 16. I was trying to remember what my young adult life with CF was like. Why don't I remember so much of what I had written? When I read my own entries I almost feel sorry for this girl – me. Yet I have such happy memories of my whole life. I had a loving Mom and Dad who were devoted to showing us love and attention, two of the best sisters who were so much fun and were like best friends, loving grandparents, Uncle Gary and Aunt Marlene and all my cousins who were more like friends than family and a neighborhood of friends that everyone envied. I knew how fortunate I was.

I honestly think that drama, trauma and trouble were games I played in many ways. I know all teens probably go through strange periods in life where they feel awkward and just want to be accepted, so in turn they may act out in crazy ways. But I took it to a whole new level. As I read some of my diary entries today I kept repeating, "What was I thinking? What was wrong with me?" I'm sure the answer was centered around the denial of my eventual fate in life with CF and wanting so badly to be accepted and needed. That is the only thing that fed my scared heart.

After being diagnosed officially with CF, I made a subconscious decision to ignore my health and my disease and with any luck it would just go away. I know Mom and Dad were stuck in such a tough position because they wanted me to live a normal life that was free of many encumbrances at a young age. But if I was ever to have a chance of living into adulthood, they recognized the need for me to adhere to my medical regimen. Postural drainage and clapping treatments were an integral part of my therapy in addition to all the antibiotics and breathing treatments.

Dad made a slanted cushion that was comfortable for me to lie on at an angle while they pounded my lungs. This was supposed to be a 30-minute treatment twice daily. I made it impossible for them by continually falling off the cushion, raising my legs in the air to obstruct their ability to reach me, talking on the phone while they clapped me and acting so mean they had to send me to my room. Mission accomplished!

They tried to be creative and make it fun by thinking of new ways to get me to induce coughing which was critical for keeping my lungs clear. For instance, they bought me a mini-trampoline that I jumped on while watching TV. I also took dance classes, swimming lessons, played on a softball team and begrudgingly took flute lessons. Believe it or not, it takes more air to play a flute than a tuba.

Finding a way to get me to take care of myself was futile. I did everything in my power to avoid any type of treatments which could help me live a better life. I even took up smoking around age 16 or 17. Thankfully I didn't like the taste or the smell of it so it was a bad habit I dropped a couple of years later (or traded in for more bad habits). The thought of hurting myself makes me sad to think about now.

As you know I learned to drive at a young age. The legal driving age is 16 in Missouri but I wanted to make sure that by the time I turned 16, I was an accomplished driver. That birthday opened up a whole new avenue for me to defy death for many years to come. Along with driving came so many new adventures - sneaking out at night and going joy riding, speeding, excessive parking tickets and having the freedom to drive to a job which gave me plenty of gas and play money. I also accumulated friends who needed a friend who could drive.

Yes, I became a magnet to friends and to the police.

I know at some point we have all watched the cop shows on TV when they take people to jail. We all say to ourselves, "What kind of person would do those things?" How about a kind, sweet Jewish gal from an upscale neighborhood with loving parents and sisters? I think I was toted to the police station over four or five times in my teens. (Thank goodness my Uncle Gary was there each time to rescue me. Mom may have left me there forever!)

For some reason I had little fear of authority. I think this is where my disease played games with my mind. I had no fear because what could anyone possibly do to me that would be worse than dying from a disease? In my mind I thought that was what lay ahead for me anyway. Death.

My very first trip to the police station was the result of driving with a false license. However I got pulled over for speeding. The officer only found the false license because I had to show him my driver's license and I didn't pull out the correct one. Back in the 70's it became very popular to go to these places that made fake drivers' licenses. All you had to do was bring in a real license of someone who was of age to drink. The backroom photographer would snap the picture of you against a monster-sized license and then shrink the whole thing to a standard size. I became my sister Mindy unbeknownst to her.

When the officer asked for my ID, I pulled out two accidentally —one of me (my real one) and the fake one with Mindy's info but with my picture. He wanted to write me a speeding ticket but couldn't figure out who I really was - Mindy or Shelly. He took me to the police station and called Mom. This is one time she was speechless. She assured the officer I was Shelly and that it was just mind-boggling how much I looked like my older sister. He wrote me tickets and let me go.

Mom drove home in silence as she welled up inside for what was going to be coming…OH NO! I knew I was in trouble because she then did the "I am so disappointed in you" speech. It would have been better if she yelled or grounded me because that was for a finite amount of time. But if she was disappointed that could last for eons and meant it would cut down on what I was allowed to do without supervision. For me it was all about living fast, living to the fullest and not slowing down. Literally. I'm not really sure why Mom and Dad put up with my defiance and never punished me severely. Maybe I kept them amused with my behavior?

Doubtful!

Being in trouble didn't scare me. I was tender and caring on the inside but developed a "You can't hurt me" steely exterior; very few things fazed me. I think this was my only way in life to deal with the inevitable. I have so many regrets about neglecting my health during this rebellious phase in my life.

I do vividly remember one of the first times I really got sick and I have to use that word because it was pretty serious. I don't know that I took it seriously though. I can tell by my old diary entry that I thought of it more as a total nuisance. I got very run down and developed a bad cold that turned into pneumonia which required me to be on IV antibiotics in the hospital. In addition to that I was also so tired; all I wanted to do was sleep. I ended up having mononucleosis which became serious enough that it affected my liver and resulted in hepatitis. All I focused on was that it was slowing me down at that moment. I never thought about what it could potentially be doing to my life span in the long run. As the weeks went by I got stronger and went back to my same lifestyle of living on the edge.

~ ~ ~

Reckless Abandon

Beth, I am finally ready to take that first step in revealing a scary chapter of my life. This leads to many more where I tried to help others and hurt myself in the process.

Writing this book has raised a lot of interesting conversations between me and my loved ones. It's interesting to recount the past 51 years of my life and take others on the journey with me. In an effort to remember many things I would like to forget, I looked through my old diaries again last night. Wow, did I go through a crazy period in life for about 20 years!

The one thing that stands out is that no matter how confusing my personal life was I always worked hard. I may have missed weeks of school or made horrible grades throughout my entire schooling but I always excelled at my job and later my career. From the day I got my first real job I never missed one day of work. There were even times when I had two and three jobs at a time simply because I loved to work. Maybe that was the one thing in life I could control and was something that built my self-esteem.

I'm not sure of the exact age when I started engaging in adult reckless behavior. Looking back it was definitely a pattern. I think a great part of it began when I denied having CF. It must have been a combination of rebellion, anger and wanting to defy death. The harder I pushed to do things that could potentially shorten my life, the more I tried to prove to myself that I was invincible. Perhaps subconsciously there was a part of me that figured "What the heck? If I'm not going to live into my twenties, why worry about anything? I'll live for the moment because the future won't be there anyway."

Mom used to jokingly say that she never knew if I would bring home a stray dog or a stray person. From grade school through high school, our home is where everyone congregated because Mom and Dad always made everyone feel welcome and like family. They were the ones that all of our friends could confide in and go to for help. I always thought I could help everyone, too, even if it meant hurting myself in the process.

That is how I entered my first real relationship when I was 17. I met a young man who was four years older, smart, good-looking, cultured and well-off financially. He always had big money in his pocket. I never questioned how someone who didn't have a job could lead such a glamorous life. I would eventually discover that all this glamour was merely smoke and mirrors to disguise a very sad life. He lived behind flash and cash to mask a life filled with drugs, deception and destruction.

Although I was very mischievous at a young age, I was not a bad girl. I was a good girl who made bad choices. Not really bad but I just pushed the limits. So when I started dating this fellow I actually thought I had found an older guy who was more stable than I. Mom and Dad had a fit when they found out his true age but I assured them he was a good choice.

It was the 70's and disco was huge. Those were the days of memberships to private disco clubs, backgammon and late night parties; unfortunately drugs were all the rage. I was not into the drug scene at this time so I didn't initially recognize a lot of the behavior of those who were.

The first year of our relationship centered around a fast-paced lifestyle with lots of expensive dinners and parties. It was all so exciting to me and I finally had what I could call a true boyfriend.

The next year I would be leaving home to attend college which meant being five hours away from him. I didn't know what was ahead in our relationship. I just knew it was fun.

After the first year I started seeing a pattern that was strange and troubling. One day my boyfriend confided that he had a drug problem and needed help; the burden was on me. I knew Mom would stop me from seeing him immediately if she knew. So I told no one.

I was oblivious and too trusting. His lifestyle didn't change despite my efforts. Because I couldn't tell anyone about this situation, I became somewhat isolated from my own friends and sadly I don't remember ever telling my sisters which is hard for me to believe because we were so close. I suppose I didn't want to drag them into my problem. I couldn't face anyone knowing that I was trapped in a bad situation. It wasn't until years later when his life became dangerously out of control that I finally realized I couldn't help him despite my caring efforts. I had to walk away.

When I left for college it now left us separated by miles and on the weekends I was driving back and forth from my college in Columbia, Missouri to the other large college town in Lawrence, Kansas so that I could spend time with "my boyfriend". The travel alone was very taxing - I would leave on Fridays after school driving close to 4.5 hours and return very late on Sunday nights. This caused me to step even further away from the College lifestyle. But what made matters worse is that my weekends were spent playing detective and psychiatrist. His parents were elderly and very wealthy and were true southerners who lived in a prestigious area of North Carolina. Kind, soft spoken and gentle.

His mother would call me often worried that she had not been able to get a hold of her son on the phone. I have to admit there were so many times that I could not either but he always had a good excuse. Study hall, tests, study groups and a part time job . It was not until the second year of our relationship that I found out he was not even enrolled in college courses. When his Mom would call she would be in tears and beg me to drive to Lawrence to check on "her boy." She was so desperate and worried that each time I would get in my car and drive hours to check on him. As a few years went by I began seeing signs of serious drug use - the kind that requires professional help to address and now a few years into our relationship, besides caring about him I felt that I had to save him. There was a naive part of me that thought "once he likes me enough, he will quit doing this." This is where you can really begin to lose a part of yourself and your confidence when you are in a sick relationship like this. You begin to blame yourself. You think that you have to make someone care about you enough so that they will change. And the worse they are the more you start to think you are not worthy. This only led to hurting myself. I became somewhat depressed, isolated due to the guilt and burden.

I felt so alone and isolated in my situation because I knew if anyone in my family knew they would demand I quit seeing him. The mental anguish of taking care of someone with a drug problem is something that you can't explain.

Our relationship finally came to an end when his mother called me one Friday and said she had not talked to her son in two days. I had not either and was worried but I had finals so it was nearly impossible for me to leave and drive to see him. Eventually I relented and agreed to drive that evening to Lawrence. When I arrived at the door of his house, a somewhat familiar stranger answered the door. I recognized this guy because he had been involved in a drug-related missing person's case. What struck me most odd is that when the missing person's case was in the paper, they also tied it to a robbery. They showed some of the missing pieces of jewelry which the person (who was missing) owned. One of the rings was on the finger of this guy. My knees buckled and I felt sick—something was very wrong. I looked and saw my boyfriend slowly walking down the stairs of his cold big house and in the reflection of one of the mirrors I could see the house was in shambles. The kitchen looked destroyed . He came to the door and looked at me with sad eyes and said I would have to leave right now. He looked desperate, scared but serious. He did not want me there. I walked away from the door and headed back to my car. But I knew something was wrong and I couldn't leave. I walked back to the house and opened the door and walked inside. I cannot describe the scene when I entered but I knew I had to help. I grabbed my boyfriend by the arm, grabbed his two samoyed dogs and literally dragged them to my car. The other fellow was still left in the house. My boyfriend was out of it so I got little resistance. I am not sure he was even breathing. I drove to a pay phone and called Mom. In two minutes, I summed up my three years of silent pain.

Mom said she would kill me later but now we had to deal with the situation at hand. She made a call to a psychiatrist in Kansas City who said for me to drive him to the hospital in Kansas City (which was about an hour away) and she also called my boyfriend's mother in North Carolina and she agreed to have him admitted to the psych ward. Mom met me at the hospital and we checked my boyfriend in while we took the two dogs to our house. That was the only part of this story that was funny to me. Mom was not a dog lover and as a matter of fact we never had one dog in our house growing up. Too much hair and dirt. Now we had two, big, furry shedding dogs in our home. THIS was the biggest sacrifice mom would have to make. Within the week, his brother came into town and picked up the dogs.

What is hard to believe is that there was a part of me that still felt responsible for my boyfriend. I felt like I could not abandon him-even at this point. Mom told me to give it a month and once he finished treatment, I may feel differently. She told me to trust her- that the person I knew and thought I cared about would not even be the same person who emerged from treatment and that he still had a long way to go before he would be OK. She was right. As time went by, my feelings did change. I was now separated enough from the situation to see how sick I had become. How much of his problem became my problem and slowly took my own life away. I thought that this would be a lesson in life I would never forget- guess I was wrong.

As I look back I realize how naïve I was. You would think I would have learned a valuable lesson from all this but I didn't. I continued making poor decisions in my personal life and academic life. Only much later in life did I realize that only those who want to be saved have the ability to save themselves.

~ ~ ~

The Young Saleslady

Fortunately for Shelly and some of her friends, their high school offered a program where students could leave school at 10:30 and go to work. They had to maintain a 20-hour work week in order to qualify. Of course Shelly signed up for this opportunity; it seemed too good to be true from her perspective.

She secured a job at a very high-end department store selling clothing in the junior department where she was paid an hourly wage along with a commission on sales. She absolutely loved it. Her interest in fashion was a reflection of having grown up around the industry. She even majored in fashion design in college and might have gone on to pursue a career in this field were it not for failing her sewing project for the year when she cut out a dress pattern incorrectly and was forced to choose a new major.

She relished in helping customers put together outfits and accessories and quickly discovered that she could outsell any of the other associates. She especially loved the competition when coworkers made up contests among themselves by picking out something hideous to wear and challenging one another to be the first to sell it. Shelly always won and did so with ease. As she continued to sell more and more, her commission checks grew and that translated into having more money to spend partying on weekends.

The buyer for her department recognized her innate ability in sales and quickly made her a junior assistant buyer which was quite an honor since she was only part-time. This 17-year-old teenager embraced the opportunity to review new lines of apparel, help with the scheduling and hiring of new employees and oversee the work of experienced ladies who were twice her age and more.

Working was Shelly's priority and selling was her passion. It really didn't matter what it was. She could sell it. This did not go unnoticed by one of her regular customers, a lady who owned a successful typesetting business that produced newsletters, ads, signs, etc. Many of the top-end advertising agencies and stores in Kansas City used this lady's services to prepare their ads and copy. The owner offered to hire and train Shelly in this field of expertise and put her in a starting sales position.

The only problem was that Felicia and Seymour insisted Shelly go to college for more formal education. As much as Shelly preferred working over attending classes, she respected her parent's position on this because the majority of companies in big business only hired those with college degrees. When she reluctantly turned down the position, the owner promised that the job would still be there for her if or when she came home from college. This would be sooner rather than later although no one knew it at the time.

~ ~ ~

College and Controversy

Shelly didn't feel like she fit in at college from the start. She still had to deal with CF and it was during this time that she was first aware of the disease starting to affect her life in a negative way. It was becoming harder to breathe and she had bouts of pneumonia, fevers and fatigue. Even though Felicia found a doctor in the area who could treat Shelly's symptoms, she had no intentions of doing her breathing treatments regularly or following the doctor's orders.

The first year of school was not easy and Shelly hated everything about it. She did the mandatory sorority rush by going around to the different sorority houses, meeting all the girls and waiting to see if she was invited back. Although the whole process was nothing more than an adult popularity contest in her mind, she joined the one sorority that invited her back.

Once she got into the sorority lifestyle, she realized it really didn't fit her personal lifestyle or desires. Yes, it was nice to have a group of girls she could call "family" while away from home but it was very cliquish. It was certainly nothing like her family at home. There were so many events planned around the clock and at all hours of the night that it left her very little time to study (which she had trouble doing anyhow) and do her meds (which she had even more trouble doing). She did find time, however, to eat pizza, popcorn, candy bars and knishes from the local deli. In no time at all she had put on the proverbial 'freshman fifteen.' Fifteen pounds on top of what was already excess weight was not a desirable look in her eyes.

She eventually stopped going to the sorority functions and found that making her own friends in the dorm was just as satisfying. Dorm life provided some fun, especially being involved in a panty raid when she joined all the girls who were hurling their underwear out the windows. The idea was to put their phone numbers on the intimate apparel and when the guys caught them, they'd call. What Shelly didn't think about in advance and later regretted was that she should have had a backup pair of size 4 underpants (as opposed to her size 12+) so she at least had a fighting chance. As all the tiny pairs of underwear soared quickly to the ground, she painfully watched hers open up like a parachute and slowly float through the air for what seemed like an eternity before landing. Her phone never rang.

She elected not to do any breathing treatments for the first several months. Each time her parents called they would ask, "Shelly, are you doing your meds? You swear?" She assured them she was but they never believed her. After three months of lying, they told her they knew she hadn't been doing her treatments or she would have seen the money her dad had hidden inside the nebulizer box to surprise her. Lying had become more than a bad habit; it had become a quick escape route. It was the only option in Shelly's mind to shield her parents from more disappointment in her. It seemed like the path of least resistance. Instead it was the path of destruction as her disease continued to pillage her body.

~ ~ ~

All Work and All Play

After Shelly's dismal first year away at college, it was a very easy decision for her to return to Kansas City and go to a local junior college. She was sporting a whopping 1.9 GPA and was completely wasting her time and her parents' money. Typically she had a perfect plan in place. She could enroll in minimal classes, slowly bring up her GPA and get a job at the same time. She knew exactly who to call – the woman who said she'd hold a job for her in the typesetting industry. While Felicia and Seymour were supportive of Shelly's work ethic, they were upset that she wasn't taking her education more seriously. After hours of pleading her case, she finally wore them down. She assured them she could be successful with or without a college degree and was determined to prove her point.

Returning home to live with her parents was not a big adjustment; she had always enjoyed being with them and was never embarrassed to admit this to her friends. If anything it may have been an adjustment for them to have her back home with the late hours she kept.

Coming home was actually the best thing that could have happened at this period in her life because she joined a fitness center. For the first time in her life, she was determined to lose weight and take control of her image. Although it wasn't easy to work out due to her lung condition and the intense coughing that ensued, she began to notice that she could actually breathe better.

Under duress she enrolled in a local community college in Kansas City. She only took a few courses because she wanted to work as much as possible. Her mind was completely consumed with contacting the owner of the typesetting company as soon as possible. As promised, this lady had kept a job open for her in the sales department.

Shelly immediately said "Yes" to the opportunity of having her first official job with a 40-hour work week, an office, an expense account and a salary plus commission. While many people might have shied away from commission-oriented work, it was a must for Shelly. It was an incentive to be the best in a small company that she envisioned growing.

She quickly adapted to the 9 a.m. to 4 p.m. working day and begrudgingly went to school a few nights a week. More importantly she had the weekends free which meant plenty of time to party with friends. Within a few weeks she quickly learned the business of print and typesetting and felt comfortable venturing out on her own and making sales calls. She loved the freedom of having the entire city as her territory opposed to being limited to a certain market or area.

As she spent countless hours making cold calls, she started identifying a few key markets which did steady business in typesetting. Once she realized that hospitals and ad agencies were big producers of print newsletters and ads, she became a self-proclaimed expert in these two fields and learned all she could about their needs. She had no fear of making inroads quickly and went right to the top people with the biggest accounts.

Without hesitation she made her first sales call with the largest ad agency in town. She met with an older gentleman, John, who said he would give her a chance of securing a big order if the quote was competitive. Shelly went into action, spent many days on the project and mailed the quote along with a note of thanks.

Two days later her note was returned with red editing marks that highlighted all the spelling, punctuation and grammar errors she'd made. John added an additional note that read: "I hope this shocks you and embarrasses you so that you pay attention to detail and never make these types of mistakes with anyone else again."

She was mortified. However, the envelope also included a very large purchase order for two jobs. John's note was a defining moment in her budding career. From that point on she learned how to hustle, multi-task and pay attention to detail. Her boss was delighted because the company could charge outrageous amounts for overtime work on the huge jobs. As she continued to excel there for three years, her checks grew larger and this 20-year-old saleswoman discovered ways to work less and make more money.

Shelly's office was an oasis of privacy she had all to herself. Around the corner was a deluxe hotel with a gorgeous roof-top pool she couldn't resist. The coy sun goddess took advantage of this decadent opportunity by flirting with the cute doormen and occasionally dating one of them. In no time at all she began wearing her bathing suit to work under her fashionable business suits. It was the perfect vain scheme. During her lunch she would drive to the hotel, have the valet park her car, leave her business suit in the locker, lie in the sun for an hour by the pool and shower before returning to work. With no one overseeing her at work, the one-hour lunches often turned into three-hour breaks or more. She was making money for the company and was on commission, so no one asked any questions.

One day she got a call from an individual who worked for the largest typesetting company in Kansas City that had all the big department store accounts and did business with many of the ad agencies. The gentleman prefaced his call by telling Shelly he learned about her stellar work when he lost one of his ad agency accounts to her. While she was reluctant to leave her job and the friendships she had established with coworkers, she was presented with an offer she couldn't refuse.

This meant saying goodbye to her job and to the cute doormen at the hotel. It was also time to say goodbye to college. She was simply not interested and wanted to devote her time and skills to making money and building a career. She told her parents that she envisioned herself getting off airplanes, holding a briefcase and being famous for something. She wasn't sure what that 'something' might be but she was certain she could make a name for herself and secure a career that would prosper without a college education. Naturally Felicia and Seymour were disappointed in her decision to quit school. They did, however, have faith in Shelly. They raised their daughters with this unconditional support even when they disagreed with some of their decisions. Knowing she had her parents' blessing inspired her even more to follow her heart.

She went to work for the new company and did very well immediately. However, after selling typesetting for nearly five years, she grew bored. Because she had free time in the evenings and on weekends, she took a job as a waitress part-time at a high-priced restaurant in the city. She thought this would be a way to meet people, make good money on tips and stay out of trouble. Her hopes of staying out of trouble were short-lived.

~ ~ ~

Blindsided by Another Ruthless Enemy

By now Shelly was devoted to exercising and running which had a dramatically positive effect on her lungs. Although she would cough uncontrollably each time she ran, she was certain she could breathe easier. She was also losing weight as a result of being conscious of her diet and health. When she dropped at least 20 pounds, she began to like the way she looked for the first time in her life. She even began studying nutrition and became a certified personal trainer.

Her change in appearance didn't go unnoticed by the opposite sex either and she enjoyed the ensuing compliments and attention.

Once she began her breathing treatments on a regular basis, her overall health improved. However, one of the many unfortunate things about having CF is becoming sick in spite of taking care of one's self. Every year or two Shelly was admitted to the hospital for a 'tune-up' which is a critical component in CF care that helps clean out some of the bacteria in the lungs and possible infections.

Shelly knew the drill; she would be given a round of intravenous (IV) antibiotics for 7-10 days. This required having a PICC line (peripherally inserted central catheter) which is a flexible tube surgically inserted into the forearm and threaded to the largest vein going to the heart which ensures receiving the maximum dosage. Due to the strength of the antibiotics, a local IV site is not possible because the drugs could burn the veins.

Once the PICC was inserted, Shelly's body was barraged with heavy-duty drugs for 3-5 days until the medicine levels were regulated. Then she was dismissed to go home and begin the around-the-clock IV antibiotic therapy. This involved hooking up 2-3 different bags of antibiotics which were alternated every 6-8 hours. When the drugs were not dripping into her veins, she flushed the IV line to keep it from clotting; while her drugs were stored in the refrigerator, it was imperative to prepare them to be delivered at room temperature. It was also important to prep the tubes to eliminate any air bubbles in the line which could potentially go into the heart.

Like others battling CF, Shelly could not permanently get rid of the bacteria in her lungs that can often grow into staphylococcus bacteria which can come and go in patients. She always remembered the hopeful tone in her doctors' voices, however, when they said, "You are lucky because you are not growing 'pseudomonas' which you don't want to have."

While in her 20's, Shelly's luck ran out when she was admitted to the hospital for a tune-up. She tested positive for pseudomonas, a type of bacteria that clings to the cell lining of the lungs, does not go away and leads to lung damage which results in a shortened life span. It can also be difficult to control because it becomes resistant to different antibiotics and then becomes hard to treat.

Shelly clearly remembered thinking, "This is the kiss of death I needed to avoid and now I have it." She also remembered the look of worry in her parents' eyes. They were always so strong that if they were worried at all, she knew she should worry, too. Instead, this new enemy that had invaded her lungs only fueled her desire to push harder and not necessarily in the right direction.

~ ~ ~

The Cocktail Waitress

Even though she was extremely busy during the day with her full-time sales job, Shelly always thought being a waitress in the evenings and on weekends sounded fun. She applied at a nearby restaurant and was hired as a cocktail waitress in the lounge area. This seemed like a good plan initially; the lounge, however, was open until midnight and all the waiters and waitresses frequently got together after work and met for a drink before going home. This meant staying out to 1 or 2 a.m. and having to get up early the next day for work. Instead of listening to her tired body that was begging for more rest, she partied with her friends.

Included in this group of friends was a tall, good-looking bartender with a wonderful sense of humor. Shelly didn't find him particularly funny one night, however, when she handed him an order for five Piña Coladas and he said, "I'm not making those. They take too long and I'm already backed up with orders. Tell the customers to order something else." Then he laughed and walked away. While some women might have shied away from a curt response like this, she was intrigued and determined to get to know him. Her curiosity was piqued even more when she learned he was working part-time and attending dental school.

After many months of working together, they started dating.

Shelly remained in dark seclusion about her disease and told no one. Instead she did whatever she could to keep pace with the inane level of partying. She had become a consummate actress in hiding how she was feeling physically and never missed a day of work in spite of her night life that was swirling out of control. As her monthly sales grew so did her commissions. After two more years at this job she was ready for a new venture.

~ ~ ~

The Competitor

At the age of 23, Shelly applied for a job with Xerox which was the leading copier company in the world at that time. She made it through the first two rounds of interviews that required selling a 'widget' to the sales manager; this was a made-up item that didn't exist but the applicants were required to put together a sales plan, a marketing plan and a sales pitch. She scored the highest out of 30 candidates.

These 30 people then went through some grueling interviews with the regional vice president of sales. The goal was to make it through the interviews and be among the final 11 candidates who would then attend a rigorous training school in Virginia for two weeks. When Shelly got to the final interview with the VP of sales in Kansas, it was brought to everyone's attention that she did not have a college degree. No one was sure how this went unnoticed but due to her strong sales background and history of success, she was given permission to attend. If she passed the course and was hired, her contract would stipulate that she would enroll in college courses while employed by them to satisfy company regulations.

The course work was held in an underground building with no windows. This alone might have intimidated some but Shelly reveled in the atmosphere. The intended new hires were in class from 7-5 every day, had evening assignments and were required to work in groups in a lab setting. They were tested every Wednesday and Friday and if they didn't score at least a 95% they were sent home without a job. This training school was also used by the largest phone company in the world at that time as well as other Fortune 500 companies.

There were 2500 young people there from Canada and the US who were all taking this course. Half were new hires for Xerox and the other half were in sales training for the large phone company. Shelly loved the competitive atmosphere of being underground with this many people who had no amenities other than a gym, a place to eat and a place to sleep. The days were filled with intense training and the nights with group studies. She welcomed the pressure and passed again with the highest score. The bad news was the detrimental toll it took on her body that was extremely worn down. By the time she returned to Kansas City she was very ill. She was certain she had pneumonia and she was right.

While excited by the prospects of returning home to see her boyfriend and beginning her new job with Xerox, she knew she needed to be in the hospital for a week of meds and treatment. She was mentally torn at this point. Her first week back from training would require traveling with a tenured rep and making cold calls which sounded exhausting because she had a fever and knew her lungs needed some serious attention. So she did the only thing she could think of in order to get a week off from her new job without having to divulge her illness.

She called in and said she had broken some toes while water skiing at the lake over the weekend. This way she could go to the hospital without anyone knowing. After finally convincing even herself that this lie was in everyone's best interest, she called her bosses and nervously explained her unfortunate dilemma.

The next day Shelly received a bouquet of flowers and a card from her new employer wishing her a speedy recovery and a lovely heart-felt note from her new boss. She felt so badly about this lie that after being released from the hospital and returning to her first week back at work, she combined purple and green eye shadow with ink from a cartridge pen and applied it to her two middle toes; this only somewhat eased the guilt she was feeling.

~ ~ ~

The Top Dog

The first weeks back at the company were extremely busy. Even though Shelly had so much to learn in stressful days filled with studying, traveling and sales calls, she enjoyed returning to both jobs and being back with her boyfriend. Her daytime job, however, was in the Kansas suburbs and she lived in the neighboring Missouri suburbs. Her waitress job was in the heart of the city so she had a great deal of driving to do every day and evening.

Although she enjoyed working at the same location as her boyfriend, she realized it would be beneficial to transfer to the restaurant's other location that was within two miles of her day job. This would make it easy to get off work around 5 and be at the restaurant to start work at 5:30. She also liked this location better because it had an outdoor patio that drew a better crowd in the evenings. The only negative was that the restaurant was open until 1:00 a.m. which meant she didn't finish until 2 a.m. on the nights and weekends she worked.

Her parents weren't happy that she was keeping two jobs with such brutal hours but Shelly wasn't shaken enough by their concern to change her lifestyle; she was focused on her excellent base salary, commissions on sales, a company car and an expense account. Her goal was to be the #1 salesperson in her division and she would settle for nothing less. She had pushed the limits all her life and saw no reason to stop.

Because her job required covering a huge territory, she knew it could take forever to service it effectively and still get to all her accounts on a good rotation. Her forte as a saleswoman had always been to find a niche that no one else recognized and it was just a matter of time until she uncovered the buried treasure that would reap great rewards professionally.

Typically she would bid on jobs and if she got the contract would bring the materials back to her company for copying or offset printing, depending on the subject matter. She noticed that all the law firms in her territory were generating copious amounts of legal documents that needed copied. Many of the documents were related to law suits and were either very graphic or private in content, so there were issues in taking the documents out of the law firm and back to the company's printing center. In trying to address the firms' needs, she realized that many were actually in need of on-site high speed copiers. This boded well for her because she received commissions on copier sales and all she had to do was pass the lead on to the copier sales division. The problem however was who would run all these copies, bind them and build the documents to specifications. The firms did not have the manpower. The cost of copying and preparing all these documents were always passed down to their clients but it was still a tedious job that required expert care.

Shelly worked closely with her boss and they developed a plan for an on-site package program for law firms. They put together a plan which included their renting the largest high-speed copiers available. They then set up an on-site copy room that they managed; this is where they kept track of billing, charge-backs to each attorney and produced everything the firms needed on-site. Since these services were billed back to the clients, there was virtually no cost to the law firms. They merely needed to supply a work area for Shelly's staff. The problem was solved thanks to her entrepreneurial vision and from that point on she was continually recognized as one of the top producers. Consequently her paychecks were commensurate with her substantially high volume of sales.

Even with such a demanding schedule it was not uncommon for her to work during the day, waitress that night, meet up with her boyfriend and stay out late partying. If only she had taken the time to listen to her lungs, she would have heard their dire plea:

"Shelly, we are starting to run out of breath. You are the only one who can save us."

~ ~ ~

Leaving the Nest

At the age of 25, Shelly enjoyed living with her parents, paying no rent and saving a lot of money. When her close friend invited her to share a two-bedroom apartment in the heart of the city, she weighed the pros and cons carefully. It seemed like the perfect move to make because it would cut down on her travel time to work and seeing her boyfriend.

The apartment building was located next to a hospital's helicopter landing pad. Each time a trauma patient was picked up or dropped off, the apartment structure rattled from the 40 mph wind gusts. The old eight-story building was without an elevator which also presented a challenge. Seymour promised his daughter that if she ever moved out he would throw her 200 lb. waterbed over the balcony before he'd ever move her again.

Living with her friend was fun. It was actually too much fun. Shelly and her boyfriend spent many nights partying with her roommate and boyfriend. She soon paid the price and had to be hospitalized twice in one year, in addition to having many bouts of pneumonia and IV antibiotic therapy. These consequences, however, didn't catch her off-guard as much as her boyfriend's proposal of marriage. While they had casually discussed getting married from time to time, Shelly couldn't recall that they'd mutually agreed they were ready for such a commitment.

Her attraction to him and appreciation of his kind heart and sense of humor were genuine. Her only concern was a dramatic one; they both enjoyed a fast lifestyle that she knew could potentially be harmful to her health. She rationalized that once he was a dentist their lives would slow down and she could focus on taking better care of herself.

That security blanket was gone when her boyfriend decided to quit dental school in spite of being so close to graduating. When he decided he was better suited for medical sales, a part of Shelly was scared knowing they would have to figure out the rest of their lives together. She quelled these fears by reminding herself that she had a wonderful job with Xerox. Her fiance' was outgoing and personable; he also had a strong work ethic which would translate into a profitable sales position with a successful company. What she didn't anticipate is that he would find this excellent job 200 miles away in St. Louis.

~ ~ ~

The Fairly Certain Bride

The new job in St. Louis was to begin immediately. This meant Shelly would be leaving her family, friends and a job she loved. She and her fiancé agreed that he would find a place to live and she would travel to see him on weekends until they were married. She immediately applied for a location transfer with Xerox and was extremely disappointed when she learned there were no sales openings in her division.

The next few months were spent getting ready for the wedding. She tried to be excited while trying on bridal gowns and picking out dishes and stemware; she tried to erase all doubts of uncertainty by telling herself this was the right decision in spite of the sacrifices she would be making. The wedding plans were so far underway by this point that she let the sheer excitement override her concerns which she kept to herself.

The wedding was truly beautiful and an extravagant event. Emotions ran high. It was especially difficult for Shelly's family because she was extremely thin and had not been taking of herself. She secretly harbored her family's same nervous sentiments. Was this man her knight in shining armor who would take care of her? Would he bring a stability to her life that she desperately needed?

Was she disciplined enough to take care of her own health?

As the newlyweds pulled away in the limousine for their romantic exit, Shelly looked back at her mother and dad whose eyes were filled with tears of concern. Their images were blurred by her own tears and fears. Instead of being overwhelmed by blissful newlywed emotions, Shelly yearned for the safety and comfort of her parents' arms.

~ ~ ~

A Mother's Intuition

Many mothers have mixed emotions when their daughters marry. Felicia's emotions were more than mixed. For several days after the wedding, she walked around the house hugging Shelly's wedding gown, clinging to the scents of her perfume and the saltiness of her daughter's perspiration.

Felicia and Seymour liked their new son-in-law. He was intelligent, fun and engaging in conversation. The only deterrent was that he wasn't Jewish. However, they gave Shelly more leeway on religious affiliation than they had given Mindy and Lori. They knew she had made the decision not to have children due to the further risks a pregnancy could impose on her health, so there wouldn't be religious issues in raising a child. Moreover, they knew it was an overwhelming responsibility for any young man to marry a woman with CF. Instead of focusing on their differences in religious backgrounds, they tried to convince themselves that he would devote his attention to her health. They accepted the fact that he was not a practicing Catholic and were relieved to find a Rabbi who would perform the mixed marriage.

Although Felicia liked him personally, she worried that her son-in-law would not take care of Shelly as much as he possibly could and be supportive of her emotional and physical needs. She was especially bothered by his lack of emotional validation; she felt like he didn't credit Shelly enough for her creativity and superior work ethic. Although Felicia didn't doubt his love, she felt her daughter deserved more support.

Felicia and Seymour had misgivings about the marriage. They were concerned they couldn't see a joy on Shelly's face they had seen on Mindy's the day of her wedding. They desperately hoped they were misreading her expression.

~ ~ ~

Shelly, I'm going to step aside for a bit and let you tell your story. I look forward to seeing what happens as you blaze your own trail in your personal and professional life.

Beth

~ ~ ~

Blazing Her Own Trail

After our honeymoon, I came back to Kansas City and packed up for my move to St. Louis. This was the hardest thing I had ever done. I had to say goodbye to everything I loved . . . my parents, sisters, relatives, friends and my job. It was extremely difficult to leave Mindy's kids, my niece and nephews, who I wanted to be there for as they grew up. However, a part of me was so excited to start my married life and become a grown-up. My first few weeks were emotionally very hard as I think I was coming down from the high of all the wedding and honeymoon excitement. My husband was working for a medical company and was doing very well. He was smart and a great salesman so I knew he would always be successful. I took a job with a local small copier company. This time I would be in copier sales which would be a new learning experience for me. The job was downtown so I had about a 40-minute commute each way.

At this point in my life I was now a workout fanatic. I went to the gym every day to lift weights and run 3-5 miles on the treadmill. Besides dropping about 40 pounds since college, I also found that my lungs felt so much better after I ran. Even though I would cough to the point where others thought I was either choking or sick with the latest influenza, I could breathe so well afterwards. I also started being very careful and conscious of what I ate. For the first time in my life I was slim and enjoyed how I looked. I also found a CF clinic in St. Louis and began seeing my doctor every three months, the very thing I was supposed to be doing the past 27 years. I was even doing my daily treatments. The only challenge I had was the weekends because we still had a lifestyle that was not conducive to having CF.

I found a gym that was right off the highway in midtown so I would get up around 4:30 - 5:00, head to the gym, work out and then shower before work. At 8:30 every morning, we had a "rah-rah go get 'em" sales meeting and were assigned a specific number of cold calls we had to do in person that day. We even had to bring back a business card from every call or we would not be paid. Then we were required to meet back at the office at 5:30 to go over our calls. This was so completely different than the professional environment I had just left at Xerox that I was not sure how long I would last. But I decided it would be a good stepping stone so I gave it my all.

So every day for seven months I would get in my faux wood paneled station wagon (company car) and load my copier into the back of the station wagon on a gurney (stretcher) and do my cold calls. My territory was Clayton which was a thriving yuppie high-rent business area full of high rise office buildings. I had no problems setting appointments to demonstrate my copier but closing sales was a long and slow painful process. It was not uncommon to go two or three weeks without getting a sale so it was a lot of work with very little financial reward. Plus it was such a non-glam job having to load and unload a machine, drag it out of the station wagon, wheel it down the sidewalks and into the office buildings. I think I went through 20 pair of panty hose a week from snagging them on the wheels of the gurney.

One Friday afternoon in August in 100-degree heat with 100% humidity, I dragged my machine up three flights of stairs in an office building where I was to do my demo. This was a three-story building with no elevator. I went into the empty room, set up the machine and waited. About fifteen minutes later my customer came in and said he was sorry no one notified me but they actually had to reschedule for the following week. I packed up my machine, loaded my gurney and left. I was to come back on Monday.

I had made friends with the young blonde receptionist whose exotic name was Murrae; she was the official screener. There would never be an appointment without getting past her. As she sat in her cute white mini-skirt with her pink high heels and her hair perfectly sprayed into place, I actually envied her job. It looked so much more glamorous than what I was doing that she and I got a good laugh from it. I told her I would be back Monday.

On Monday I went back and dragged my machine up to the third floor. I was now set up and ready for my big demo when Murrae entered the room and told me that over the weekend the company had moved to the second floor. I was going to have to undo my machine, reload the gurney and now drag that stretcher back down one flight of stairs and set up all over again. NO WAY!

I excused myself and told her I had to run out to my car because I had forgotten to bring in the copier paper. I said I would be right back. She and I smiled at one another in a way which indicated that she knew I was NOT coming back! I returned to my wood paneled station wagon and collected all my personal items and placed the car keys on the driver's seat floor mat. I called my boss at the copier company and told him there was an emergency, that I had to quit, that his copy machine was on the third floor of the Tyler Building and my car was parked in the lot with the keys on the mat. I felt so badly quitting because I had never quit anything. I knew my next move had to be something that I could enjoy doing for a very long time.

Everything about my personal and professional life appeared idyllic on the surface. My husband's career was soaring, we lived in a gorgeous home and I was paying attention to my health. Although my husband was intuitive and compassionate, he still didn't understand the magnitude of my disease. I blame myself for much of this because up to that point, I hadn't focused on taking care of myself. Once that finally changed, I wanted and needed him to be in sync with me. This was wishful thinking and nothing more.

By now it was the 1980's and cystic fibrosis was beginning to be diagnosed more frequently along with a growing awareness of the disease. Fortunately there was a reputable adult CF clinic in St. Louis and I was under the care of a doctor I liked and respected. This was the first time since being diagnosed with CF as a child that there was a separate adult clinic where I could find help. Until this point in time, there were still few adults living with CF to warrant an adult clinic.

This was a good sign as the average life expectancy was now approximately 23 for someone with CF. I was still beating the odds and felt very blessed considering my previous disregard for my health. This was also the first time there were some minor declines in my pulmonary function tests which measured the amount of air I could blow out quickly and then sustain. This measured lung volume/capacity and was a reliable indicator how my lungs were functioning. With the progression of my disease, these numbers would decline. I hated these tests because they didn't lie. Whether my test results were good or bad, they were a chilling reminder of my disease that would only progress in time.

I found it very hard to be around those with CF who were in the waiting room; people looked frail and thin and many relied on oxygen tanks to help them breathe. I found myself thinking, "I know how courageous these people are. Cystic fibrosis is a terrible disease. I know what they're feeling. There are days when you are just so sick of it. Times when you think how unfair it is not to feel good and live every day in fear that your life may be cut short. Days where you are sick of doing treatments and being on a regimented daily schedule."

I sometimes found myself secretly envious of people who were in remission and could call themselves "cancer survivors." I loathed living with a disease that had no remission; I loathed the heart-breaking reality that there was very little chance my health would improve over time. I felt cursed with a disease that had a plan of its own, one where the consequences were out of my control.

At this juncture in my life, one of my friends knew someone who had cystic fibrosis and mentioned that the St. Louis office was in great need of phone volunteers to raise money for an upcoming CF fund-raiser. Based on my abilities as a saleswoman, I felt I could help and agreed to volunteer a few days a week by helping with outbound calls. I developed friendships with many of the other volunteers and was later nominated to the Cystic Fibrosis Board of the St. Louis regional office.

I was especially thrilled when presented with the opportunity to speak alongside the legendary Jack Buck who sponsored an annual golf tournament to raise money for CF. As much as I loved knowing I was helping to raise money for a good cause, I eventually had to resign from working with the foundation because I couldn't emotionally handle seeing those who were sick and not doing well. It was too hard to hear the stories from friends and family members of those who were losing a loved one to this horrible disease.

The year I left, the president of the local CF chapter who was also the CEO of one of the largest pharmaceutical companies in the world spoke at our board meeting. When he said that he believed a cure was right around the corner, I found myself thinking, "In whose lifetime do you think a cure will be found? I pray it is mine!"

~ ~ ~

No Time for Pity

Shelly, it's hard to fathom how you've worked so hard since you were a young girl to keep your disease a secret. Harboring your feelings in school must have been excruciating many days. Harboring your secret as an adult had to be emotional torment many days, didn't it? Yet you've never sounded bitter or resentful that you were born with unhealthy lungs that would never get better. You've never considered surrendering to a disease that wants to limit and define you. Where have you found your strength to defy this malicious foe that is determined to beat you but can't because you won't relent?

~ ~ ~

Overcoming the Barriers

Beth, I have always been somebody who responds very negatively to being told "No" or "You can't do that." I always will be. When I hear that I can't do something, I'm more determined than ever to prove I can. For me, limitations are barriers that must be overcome.

I'm like that child who is told she can't have the ice cream cone she wants. Instead of accepting "no" for an answer, I loiter around the ice cream stand, promise my mother all sorts of chores in exchange for the ice cream or enlist the aid of my sisters to get it. I am like that child who will do anything rather than accept I simply can't have it.

That's not to say that as a young girl I wasn't aware of CF and the effect it would have on my life. I was just determined to prove that it would not be the dominant factor that would force me to live a life I couldn't envision. I knew what I wanted and being told that my disease might prevent me from gaining that was the counterbalance I needed to achieve it.

My experience has not only defined who I am but has given me much empathy for others who either through illness, emotional problems or other issues feel different from everybody else. I want to tell them, "You have a personality, a sense of humor, a connection to people and a life force that is separate from this other thing. Use that!"

~ ~ ~

No Such Thing as Luck

Beth, I believe there is no such thing as luck. I believe that people run into luck every day and let it slip right by them. They don't hear the cues, don't see the opportunities and don't think outside the obvious. I do think we all have the ability to create our own luck and this is something I've taken advantage of all my life – creating my own luck.

While attending one of the bar code industry trade shows, I met a man who also worked within the industry as the sales manager of a very large printing corporation out of Pennsylvania. I always had an affinity for the graphic arts and the printing industry due to my very first job selling typesetting and graphic design. I thought this could be my next career if I ever left the St. Louis-based bar code company.

The timing felt right so I called him and asked if there were any positions available. He arranged an interview and I flew in to meet him and the rest of the company. I loved the whole interview process and welcomed the opportunity to impress him with my successful track record in sales. By the end of the day I was offered a position in sales; however, I had to cover a very large territory which initially would include five states; my weeks would consist of flying out on Tuesdays and arriving home on Fridays. I had concerns in accepting the job but ironically it wasn't due to the hardship of travel. I could handle that. My husband still enjoyed a robust lifestyle which kept him out late many evenings even when I was home. I worried what could happen if I were gone every week.

Although I still had difficulty saying "no" to a somewhat crazy lifestyle at times, I was becoming more disciplined in taking care of myself. Running every morning was now an obsession and doing my breathing treatments and medicines had become priorities. Even though I was putting my health needs first, there was no guarantee I wouldn't get sick. With CF, a simple cold can turn into a life-threatening lung infection.

Air travel posed a personal risk because of the crowds and exposure to germs; it was a risk I was willing to take, however, because the new position looked so promising. This diverse company was able to do all forms of printing. It was so detailed and complicated and I loved everything about it. Training was to begin in Pennsylvania early the next week and I would be there for three weeks with the opportunity to fly home one time during that period.

I told the CEO who hired me that I had cystic fibrosis. (This was a big step for me because I had worked hard at my other jobs to keep my disease a secret.) He was a caring family man who was very compassionate and understanding. He was also interested in learning more about the disease. It was 1992 and yet so few people knew about CF. Many confused it with MS or other diseases with two-letter acronyms.

~ ~ ~

Something Had to Give

After my training session was completed, I returned home and saw my doctor immediately. I had chills, fever and serious trouble breathing. It felt like there were sharp needles poking my lungs with every breath I took. I was admitted to the hospital a few days later with pneumonia and pleurisy. I suspected that I was going to be admitted because I was having trouble running. This had now become my mental and physical gauge for my health. It was how I personally monitored and judged how I was doing. When I could run my nine-minute mile with ease, I was feeling good. When it became a struggle to finish and I had to stop often to cough, I knew I was not doing as well.

I don't like having visitors while I'm in the hospital. There is nothing worse than everyone sitting around looking at you, feeling sorry for you and trying to cheer you up. When I'm in the hospital, I'm not sad. I'm there to get treatments, to do whatever is required to become stronger and get back to my life. I spend my days dressed in workout clothes and refuse to wear a hospital gown. I'm only in bed when it's time to hook up my IV's every four hours. Otherwise, I am walking the hallways or catching some sun.

Due to my obsession with working out, I asked the doctor to write me orders to go to physical therapy every day and walk on their treadmill. I shocked the therapist the first time I got on it with the PICC line still in my arm and ran an all-out sprint. It was not uncommon for the hospital staff to enter my room and find me with my own rubber bands doing donkey kicks and leg raises. It didn't take long for the word to spread and soon everyone on my hospital floor knew there was no stopping me.

Into the second year of working my territory, I called on the Dr. Pepper/ 7-Up Company in Dallas. They turned me over to one of their divisions which produced IBC Root Beer. They were experiencing problems with the print abrading (rubbing off) on the bottles due to a new manufacturing process. They had been very loyal to the same bottle printers for years but there was now a younger man in charge of upgrading and changing the image of the brand. We developed a good rapport in knowing this could propel our careers if we could solve this problem.

The next few months entailed working on this project day and night until we ultimately designed a label that pushed the limits of what other printing companies had ever done. The executives and I flew to Indiana when it was time to test our new label. We all stood at the end of the line and watched as bottle after bottle emerged with the labels intact. Suddenly there was a big roar of elation as we all watched the birth of the new generation of the root beer label emerge. This was a good day!

After this success, I became a 'beverage specialist' and began traveling and working with different beverage companies in the country. By the beginning of the third year, however, I was so physically worn down from the excessive traveling and work load. I knew something had to give and it did.

One week when I returned home I was totally exhausted and felt ill. My lungs hurt, I had trouble breathing and was running a high fever. When I walked in the house, my husband greeted me and announced we would be meeting some friends at one of the local hang-outs we frequented on Friday nights for happy hour. There was no way I could subject myself to that environment and I asked him if we could just stay home. He was persistent that we had to go and could come home early. This was a promise I had heard too many times. I knew this was the crucial moment where I had to draw some boundaries if I were to live another day. I felt so sick that I wanted him to stay home with me because I was afraid to be alone. He said he loved me but was going anyway. Through tears I said, "If you go, I am going to move out in the morning." He reminded me how much we loved one another and how good our lives were together; we enjoyed travel, fine dining, the arts and a cultured lifestyle. I agreed but repeated my promise one more time. He chose to leave. At six o'clock the next morning, I took four drawers from my dresser and left the house. I never went back.

~ ~ ~

Baby Talk

Many women have asked me over the years if I'm sorry I didn't have children. I am sorry because I love children, especially little girls. I can't pass by a baby girl without wishing I could hold her, hug her, shield her and make her life happy. I really wonder if it's because deep down I know the pain that children can go through at points in their lives and I wish I could help them through it, even if I don't know them.

When I was a child, I had the best doll clothes money could buy. I would save my allowance and buy real baby pajamas and clothes for my doll. I bought real plastic baby food trays, and spoons and cups. I loved babies. I would accept every baby-sitting job available and then call Mom to come help me. I even took a job at a department store working in the infant clothing department.

However, I remember what the doctor in Philadelphia told me on my second visit. I was nearly 17 at the time. He explained that women with CF usually cannot conceive and that men with CF are usually sterile. Although I didn't react at the time, I think it must have affected the way I looked at dating and marriage because I do remember always thinking that no man would want to marry someone who couldn't have kids.

I told Mom this and she said it wasn't true; she reassured me that once I fell in love with a man, we could always look at adopting. I repeatedly voiced my opinion against this because I would want "my own" baby. It was not until I got married and raised my first puppy that I realized no matter who the birth mother is (or dog in my case) I would feel that same unconditional love as if I had given birth to the new life.

During our marriage, we wanted to have children and had begun looking very seriously at a surrogate mother situation. Although I wanted to share my love with children, I knew in the back of my mind that I would never have any. I never felt it would be fair to have a mother who could not take care of herself, let alone pledge to take care of her children forever. I was comfortable with my decision. As the months went by I dismissed the idea of finding a surrogate mother. I was coming to the conclusion that my husband and I might be headed toward ending our relationship which proved to be true.

~ ~ ~

Life Begins Again

The day I walked away from my marriage and away from my home and dog was one of the saddest days of my life. I called my girlfriend, Marie, and asked if I could come over — for a year! I told her I had moved out, needed a friend's shoulder to cry on and a place to stay.

I felt safe asking her for help. She was one of my few friends who knew how conflicted I had been in wanting to stay married opposed to my desperate need to find a lifestyle more conducive to my health. She had been one of the few who knew each time I was hospitalized or wasn't feeling well. We loved each other like sisters, so when I called her early in the morning, she said, "Of course. Come over little muffin."

My life was a blur the first few months after moving out. It was such an adjustment to ending a relationship with someone I had cared for after so many years of being together. Since Marie was not expecting a live-in tenant, there were really no accommodations for all my belongings.

We set up a make-shift office in her basement and cleared an extra bedroom upstairs for me. I remember going through the motions of life and thinking this was happening to someone else. There were days, maybe months, where I just sat and stared at the basement walls and cried. I'm not sure if I was mourning the loss of a love or the fear of being alone and starting over.

I knew this move was a major turning point and realized my life felt frighteningly out of control. I had spent the last years of my life running and running but not slowing down long enough to think about living. Perhaps my priorities were in the wrong place. My past life had been focused on ignoring my health and doing just about everything I could to avoid taking care of myself. Now I was forced to slow down, reorganize my priorities and my future. I needed a new plan that addressed the reality of my disease that would only get worse with time. The years I had spent abusing my body had begun to catch up with me and I had to do something to save myself. No one else could save me anymore than I could save others. I had to want to change.

At first I was having trouble even being productive at my job which I loved. Sales were soaring and I had no problem making and exceeding my quota each quarter. However, I was having trouble concentrating on anything too long. I spent hours every day pondering the same questions: Did I do the right thing? Did I give up too soon on the marriage? What if he is sad and lonely without me? I was feeling so much pain and guilt thinking I had hurt someone else.

The day I officially moved all my belongings out and the movers were loading the truck, my husband was holding me and kept repeating that we loved each other and this couldn't happen. It was tugging at my heart but history told me things would not change. On the morning of the divorce, we went to court together. Prior to that, we had already divided our things one by one: the house, the stocks, the furniture, the cookware . . . everything down to our dog we both loved dearly. I couldn't justify taking our dog away from him so I agreed to have visitation rights only. After the judge granted our divorce, he and I hugged and had breakfast together. We truly were friends who cared for one another.

Time began to heal the wounds and my life began to get back in order. However, the toll that all the stress had taken on my health manifested itself in strange ways. I had horrible stomach pains, my lungs were hurting and for the first time I could remember, I sporadically coughed up blood a few times within a year. It took my breath away each time it happened. I was so scared that it made me slow down and ask myself, "Could I be declining?"

In following my necessary protocol for treatments, I did my usual 14 days of IV antibiotic PICC line therapy to help knock down my lung infections. I also had my third sinus surgery which came as no surprise; it is very common for people with CF to have multiple sinus surgeries in their lifetimes. The resident bacteria manifests in the sinus cavities and the sinuses become totally blocked. At that time, my doctors performed a procedure called 'windows' by cutting out a pathway in my maxillary sinus. It is not the natural path and this method isn't even used anymore. There is a new procedure that has replaced the old one but at the time they found this to be most effective. The problem is that over time you have a build-up of scar tissue and more bacteria, so the cycle begins all over and it becomes necessary to have multiple surgeries. The one significant positive in my life is that I was making a conscious effort to take care of my health and do my daily breathing treatments. It seemed to be paying off as my pulmonary functions remained relatively stable.

~ ~ ~

A New Venture

Being single was a new experience for me and I wasn't sure I liked it. It did, however, provide a great deal of free time. I did the necessary traveling during the week that was exhausting physically and on weekends I would go out with Marie or other friends. I had a few dates here and there but nothing that seemed too promising. I was actually a little bored with my life and decided to look for a part-time job; something that would be fun, challenging and possibly lead to a new career.

While driving around one day, I stopped at my favorite local Chinese restaurant. It was set up for take-out orders only. I started talking to the owner who was a young guy and he shared that he wanted to open a second location. I don't know what possessed me to consider opening a restaurant but I told him I would like to look at being his partner. We went through months of bantering around ideas, looking at locations and meeting with architects.

Things actually seemed to be making sense. I would be a financial partner while traveling during the week and a working partner on the weekends.

This was the same year there was so much rain in St. Louis that the levee broke, flooded and devastated an entire area of Missouri stretching hundreds of miles. Businesses and homes were completely lost. This must have been a sign from above because the future restaurant location we were considering was wiped out as well.

I was now at a point in my life where I wanted my own home and purchased one in an exclusive area in West County. This was a well-established and safe area where many successful business people and their families lived. My neighbors, who were working professionals, had two younger children I enjoyed so much. I was really excited about my new house and wanted it to reflect something fresh and unique. I picked out what I thought to be two very contemporary contrasting colors; one for the house and one for the shutters and door. I left town to visit some friends in

Chicago and when I returned my house was painted. What I thought was a lovely peach shade was pink and what I thought was a complimentary gray color for the shutters was green. My house was now pink and green. As I pulled into the driveway, I was greeted by my new neighbors, Dale and Linda, who had barely spoken two words to me as of yet. Dale walked up to my garage and in his deep roaring voice said, "You are NOT thinking of leaving it that color, are you?"

This was the start of 10 years and counting of wonderful friendship. Linda told me Dale worked in the beauty business industry and was a manufacturer's rep for big companies that sold beauty supplies to salons. I shared that I was entertaining the idea of opening my own business in my spare time and would look into the beauty business as an option.

I started paying attention to the salons in St. Louis and saw a new trend emerging: a large salon with an attached beauty super store that carried multiple lines of hair care, skin care, nail polish and every incidental beauty product imaginable. I loved this idea because it was a business that was sales driven and selling was one thing I knew how to do. I spent the next few weeks looking around and wandering in and out of salons, talking to owners, customers and landlords. This was an exciting industry but a total departure from selling printing and I knew I had a lot to learn. What would also make it challenging is that I would keep my other job at the same time. I was determined to move forward with my plan no matter what. I just had to figure out how. By now I was 34 years old.

~ ~ ~

A Beauty Queen is Born

I had been playing the single game for at least a year and found that most guys my age were all the same. They seemed like good guys but were still into the bar and party scene. This was something I now wanted to distance myself from as much as possible. I was introduced to a fellow through some mutual friends. He was very soft spoken and somewhat quiet. He was from a good family and was very close to his parents, brother and sister. I liked his strong family ties. He had a fairly strict Catholic upbringing and although it was completely the opposite of my Judaic background, I liked the fact that he was stable. He had a basic job, a basic car, a basic personality and was a basically good guy. Suddenly, basic seemed like a refreshing change.

I think at the time it was so juxtaposed to my previous relationship that something more sedate and almost boring was appealing to me. He also had three fantastic children from a previous marriage and I felt a connection with the kids the first day I met them, especially the little girl. I think because I had no children and always wanted a little girl of my own, it made me all the more attracted to the situation. I told him about my health issues and although he showed concern, I am not sure he really understood the challenges that he may eventually face.

Since I was always one to mask any bad days I had, I don't think he saw how my health affected me during the first few years of our relationship. There were also new treatments for CF patients in the 1990's and with the introduction of a new drug called Pulmozyne (which I think has been a life-saver for me) I could do more to help take care of myself at home. The cost of treating CF is astronomical between the insurance (if one can get it), the monthly drugs which can run in excess of $5,800/month (co-pays help ease the burden) and the expense of home care nursing and drugs during all home IV therapy treatments.

I also began using a new breathing therapy device that looked like a ski vest. I hooked one end of a hose to the vest and connected the other end to a motor. The force of the air generated from the motor shook my body rapidly to move the secretions in my lungs to keep them as clear as possible.

After a few years of dating, we both wanted our own business and decided we'd make good business partners. He liked the idea of opening a retail beauty spa and was comfortable being a working partner; he had enough flexibility in his current career to do this. One day I walked into a small shop at a busy local strip center within a mile of my home. It was the hub for every essential store you need in a neighborhood with the largest grocery chain in St. Louis, a dry cleaners, a pizza pub, a barber shop and a St. Louis Bread Company. It also had a small 900 sq. foot hair salon that catered to what we used to call the "blue hair, martini crowd."

This salon had been in the same location forever and serviced over 200 ladies who came in every week for a shampoo and set. Each one walked out with the same color of blue hair and the same pouffed hair-do which was lacquered to last one week without washing. The salon had a very loyal customer base and the stylists and customers were all like family to one another. I met with the owner to ask about the business and she said, "You can have it." She was having health issues and was more than ready to sell the salon. My timing was perfect. She wanted $35,000 for the business which was yielding a nice profit every year.

Since this was not going to be my full-time career and just a little side business, I wasn't dependent on it for financial support. However, I did not have $35,000 that I was able to part with since I had just bought a house. With no equity in my home as of yet there was no way I would qualify for a loan. I could apply for a small business loan which was popular at the time and easier to get but time was of the essence. I really wanted this business and didn't want to delay in making an offer.

I returned home to Kansas City and sat down with Mom and Dad. Prior to that I had prepared a business plan indicating how the salon was currently doing and how I would change it to become more profitable. I had an estimate of how much it would cost to renovate and change things so it could accommodate shelves for retail space to be added in front. This is the part I was most interested in anyhow; I also knew how much I needed for start-up inventory.

Mom and Dad had always been open-minded about anything with which I had approached them and even though I had a history of making bad personal choices, they always had the utmost faith in my business savvy. They offered to put up their home as collateral. They also voiced the same concern: How would I travel and also run a new business? I promised I would make it work. One advantage I had is that I was able to assume the lease of the current salon owner, so I was grandfathered in for seven years at an excellent rate per square foot. This meant I better like this business for a long time.

I started by hiring a good friend, Joe, to renovate the salon which involved moving stations, adding chairs, setting up shelves and shelves of products and taking out the waiting room which did not go over well at first. With customers having no place to sit and wait, they were forced to walk around and shop. I also changed the name to something that suggested to casual passers-by that it was more than a salon, that it was also a place to purchase products. I called it 'The Beauty Source.'

By now my boyfriend and I were living together. I kept up with my day job and worked at the salon on weekends and evenings. We would travel as often as possible to see his children and had them stay with us for long weekends and holidays. I loved having them and enjoyed the feeling of being together as a family.

My salon business was growing rapidly and I was attracting more new stylists who wanted to work for me. I found myself wanting to spend all my time at the salon and began to dread leaving town each week with my other job. We were making a good profit and that included paying a full-time manager to be there in my absence. I realized it was time to make a bold move and leave my printing career so I could commit full-time to my salon. I knew this was the only way to grow my business to full potential. Calling the vice president of the company and telling him I would be leaving was one of the toughest calls I made in my professional career; I dearly loved what I was doing and enjoyed my coworkers. They reluctantly accepted my resignation and asked that I stay an extra month to train my replacement.

~ ~ ~

One Thing Leads to Another

Now that I was relying on the salon to generate my income, I felt like I needed a bigger plan. There was a Mail Boxes Etc. store next door to my salon. We did a great deal of business there, the location was always busy and the owners were elderly and ready to retire. They made me a very attractive offer so I used some of the assets of the salon to secure a small business loan and bought the store. The plan was that my boyfriend would primarily run this business which I thought would work out well. However, when it came time for us to go to San Diego for the mandatory two-week National Franchise Mail Boxes Etc. training school, I was the only one who went for training. It made me question his commitment to the business.

I soon realized that I needed to expand 'The Beauty Source' which was doing very well. I had more stylists wanting to work for me than I could accommodate but in order to grow, I needed a strong partner. I talked to my neighbor, Linda, who was now my best friend and asked if she would like to buy into half of my business and expand our first location as well as open another location. After a great deal of brainstorming, we sealed the deal.

There was a large 4000 square foot floral shop going out of business in our same strip center and we were able to grab that location. We were going from 900 square feet to 4000 and now with a partner to split the profits, the pressure was on to grow quickly. At the same time this expansion was underway, we found a smaller salon in the southern part of the city that also had some of the same type of anchor tenants we had in our primary location.

We made a deal with the owner and bought that salon which became another location of 'The Beauty Source.' Now things were really hopping and business was booming. Linda and I were like a fine-tuned machine in running our stores. We had promotions, sales contests, incentive trips, on-going education opportunities and clever marketing strategies that brought in more new customers than we could serve. We also had a waiting list of stylists who wanted to work for us. I hated to pass up business, so if there was a way to add stylists to our staff, I would find somewhere to put them even if it meant hanging their stations from the ceiling!

Linda and I were having so much fun and there was never a dull moment when working with people who were so creative. The word soon spread in St. Louis that 'The Beauty Source' was the place to work and go to for services. We became the official salon for the St. Louis Rams cheerleaders and were honored as one of the fastest growing salons in the country by the industry's top trade magazine. We had a salon owner from another prominent area of town approach us to buy her salon and soon the third Beauty Source was open. This shop was close to 9000 square feet. We opened a 20-bed tanning salon next door and now had everything our customers needed for personal beauty care all under one roof. Our spa business was really booming and skin care services were rapidly becoming the driving force in our shops.

The Mail Boxes Etc. store was a great deal of work but also very profitable. There was another Mail Boxes Etc. Store which was for sale near our third Beauty Source location so it only made sense to buy that one as well. Because the businesses were doing so well, I was able to establish a solid relationship with a bank and could use my assets from one location to secure a loan for the next one.

My health seemed stable at this point. Perhaps the lack of rigorous travel was working in my favor. Things seemed to be going well in my personal relationship as well and I was doing what I loved. As the next few years went by, I was spending most of my time running the salons but still working closely with the store managers of our Mail Boxes Etc. stores to make sure they were running smoothly.

I started noticing that my boyfriend spent more and more time working in the Mail Boxes Etc. store, especially the one which was further from our house. I was happy about that as I thought it would help keep things on track. Linda and I became inseparable and when we weren't working, we would sneak away for a few hours to enjoy golf which had become my new addiction. Everyone found it pretty amazing that she and I could be business partners, neighbors and friends and never argue. We were simply a great team.

One day I was in the salon when a young gal walked in and said she was dating the owner who had offered her a day of beauty treatments. I looked at Linda and said, "She's dating Dale???" We both knew that was hardly the case. Instead she was dating my boyfriend! We both actually began laughing uncontrollably. Surprise!!! I didn't see that one coming. I was so busy, so content and so trusting that I honestly never stopped to think about anything like this happening.

The first thing that came to mind wasn't how he could do this to me but rather what about his kids? I couldn't bear the thought of saying goodbye to them.

~ ~ ~

Rebound?

When any relationship breaks down, I think it's probably normal to doubt and question yourself. Did I do something that led to this? Was it somehow my fault? I know my flaws and weaknesses and I can always take a step back and look at relationships very objectively even if I don't like seeing my own mistakes. In past relationships and in life, I was no angel; I realized I needed to change a great deal. I also realized that I had overlooked and perhaps dismissed some of my boyfriend's inconsistent and odd behavior at times.

I was now in my 30's and it never occurred to me to be concerned about my personal or professional life. I took everything at face value because life was good. I had what I thought to be a trusting and close relationship, tons of friends I cared about and who cared about me, a beautiful home and thriving businesses. My health was stable and I was feeling pretty good most days.

My girlfriend, Robyn, never had a good feeling about the relationship. She is a psychologist and maybe her instinct was sharper than mine. I'm certain what bothered her most was that every time I was admitted to the hospital for treatment, my boyfriend never came with me. She also couldn't understand how a man could live 800 miles away from his young children. I realize that should have been a red flag but for some reason I justified it.

Although I was hurt that he had cheated, I wasn't depressed or saddened. It was just over.

Maybe being with him had been a 'rebound' relationship for me from the start but I think everything in life is a rebound. We all make decisions based on our past and at the time we met, he was a change from that and a good diversion.

The challenge was how to divide the businesses. We eventually found a common ground and I gave up the Mail Boxes Etc. stores in exchange for all three of my salons and tanning spa. I did, however, give up a great deal of my savings in order to make the deal. I didn't care. I just wanted to move on with my life. My sanity and peace of mind mattered more than the money.

During our separation, he left town for a week. He was "stressed out" and needed a break. He left me to do everything- work with the real estate agent, clean up, get paperwork in order, and on and on. I was so angry that I decided to really help get our house cleaned out quickly. So while he was gone I took his prize possessions which was a garage full of premium tools, riding lawn mowers, power tools, everything a spoiled boy needs and I had a garage clearance sale. An "All things must go sale." I had it the weekend that 20 guys were resurfacing our neighborhood streets. Just the kind of boys who would appreciate a good sale on boys' toys. I sold things for pennies on the dollar. I took cash or bad checks! I even had a few buy one/get two free offers!! I was just trying to help lighten his workload when he returned.

It was emotionally difficult to close one chapter of my life and start over again but I had faith I would be just fine. The hardest part was knowing I wouldn't see his kids or family again. I know my family was sorry for me but relieved at the same time. For many reasons, they never believed our relationship would result in marriage.

After the sale of the house I moved into my own apartment nearby. This was actually the first time in my life I lived alone and I really liked it. I now had more time to focus on running our businesses and enjoyed being single. Linda and I continued to work hard; we alternated working the three locations that now employed over 110 employees and somehow continued to find time to golf. We were also very close to many of our stylists who were a wild and interesting bunch! So there were evenings and weekends filled with dinners, parties, trips and memorable times together. However, I did not abuse my health. I actually became even more committed to my health routine as well as working out diligently.

Dating again was interesting. I wasn't looking for a serious relationship and enjoyed staying busy while most of my friends were either married now or single and into partying.

Because I was so active in working, playing golf or attending social events with friends and business associates, it wasn't difficult meeting suitable men. I dated one fellow who was an avid golfer but that was not a full-time relationship for either of us. I dated another man I cared about but our backgrounds and social interests were very different. I dated guys who were extremely intelligent businessmen to those whose vocabularies were so limited I could only use single syllable words or I would lose them. I went on one disastrous blind date that required a ladder to reach the seat of the truck; this guy then lit a cigarette with the windows rolled up. If that weren't enough, the heater was broken in frigid weather conditions. I told him I had a lung disease called cystic fibrosis and being around smoke was deadly to me. His reply was, "Whoa, yeah, I've had hangovers where I thought I was going to die," as he continued to smoke. I think he missed my point!

I was also eating a lot of elegant meals, sitting in the best hockey seats, taking fantastic trips and going to ritzy black-tie functions. Dates like these made me yearn for someone special. I needed to be with a man who would provide me with a sense of security and unconditional love. After being single now for nearly three years, I started to doubt if Mr. Wonderful was really out there for me.

~ ~ ~

I Love Telemarketers

When I was married I loved cooking on Sundays. I often picked out a challenging recipe and spent a great deal of the day creating it. However, one particular Sunday I was cooking dinner for myself, playing music and sipping a white wine when the phone rang. My hands were covered with onions so I balanced the phone up to my ear to discover it was a telemarketer. Because I've been in sales my entire life, I'm more sensitive to those callers. I usually listen to their sales pitch, politely tell them I'm not interested but appreciated their efforts and wish them well.

By the time this telemarketer started talking, I had already buried my hands in raw hamburger. Although I was not really interested, she held me captive. I couldn't touch the phone with my hands to hang up so I just continued to listen. She said they were giving away free trips to Ft. Lauderdale for those who qualified and it was an all-expense paid trip for three days. In exchange I would have to take a two-hour tour of their new time-share offer. After that I was free to go. There were no strings attached and I could enjoy the rest of my free vacation on the beach. As a matter of fact, I even got $100 just for listening and could invite one person as a guest. Their air fare wouldn't be covered but they could stay and tour with me.

I don't know what possessed me to say, "Sounds good." The only caveat was I had to send a $200 down payment which was non-refundable if I didn't book the trip within one year. So here I was on a cold and gloomy day in March, 2000 thinking about this free trip to Florida where I could bask in the sun. I was a little buzzed from the wine and ready for something adventurous in my now routine life, so I gave her my credit card information and the gal said she would send me the confirmation and instructions. I had one year to use the free offer. I hung up the phone and went back to creating my masterpiece for dinner.

It was now February of 2001 and I was cleaning out my apartment in preparation to move to a larger apartment two doors down. I needed an extra bedroom so I could have an office in my home since the salons didn't have enough space. As I was cleaning out some desk drawers, I came across an oversized envelope and saw it was from the time-share company. The envelope was still sealed. I had never opened it; in fact, I had totally forgotten about the free trip I bought. It was stamped in red as being "Time sensitive material." I was hoping that meant I had a year to open it! It was my trip confirmation and I realized that I was down to the deadline and had to at least book the trip immediately.

I called one of my girlfriends, Ellen, a stylist at my shop who was single and a good friend. I knew she would welcome a chance to go somewhere warm since she was a sun goddess.

We picked a date that couldn't arrive fast enough. By now I had been divorced for two years and had absolutely no intentions of buying a property in Florida even though I always dreamed of living there. I was simply looking forward to having fun on a free vacation. That's all.

~ ~ ~

The Stoplight

When Ellen and I arrived in Ft. Lauderdale, we picked up our rental car and headed down the beautiful stretch of A1A. When we stopped for a red light, I looked to my right and saw an absolute Adonis waiting to cross the street. Our eyes met and this extremely good-looking guy said, "You are gawgeous," in a New England accent. The irony is that I am not gorgeous. I am funny, nice, loving and bubbly but certainly not gorgeous. But hey, who would pass up a compliment like that?

The light was turning green and I felt a panic come over me. If I kept going, I would never find out who this guy was. But, I would be crazy to pull over to talk to a total stranger. And, if I did, I would be breaking the #1 rule Ellen and I had made. No guys this trip. Just a girl's weekend together. But something possessed me to pull over to meet this striking man who introduced himself as Frankie Tedesco. We explained we were on vacation and had just arrived in town. He said he would be happy to show us all the 'happening spots' and told us to take his number if we ever wanted to call for suggestions. Here was a total stranger I knew nothing about and yet I sensed he was safe and genuine. I took his number, threw it in the glove box and we went on our way.

We decided to call him the following day and see what he suggested. We planned to meet at a popular place in Las Olas. As the day went on, my girlfriend and I ate too much, read in the sun and didn't feel like washing our hair or getting dressed up. So we didn't show up to meet Frankie, thinking it didn't matter much; we didn't even call to cancel. I started to feel guilty later and called to apologize. We agreed to meet again for dinner. It happened to be my girlfriend's birthday and when we arrived at the restaurant, Frankie had a decorated table waiting. Besides paying for our meals, he had a birthday cake brought to the table. I was wondering if this guy was for real. Most men this good-looking would not feel the necessity of going to so much trouble to impress a woman.

He was sharply dressed and paid for dinner with cash so part of me thought I had snagged a rich one. Yet oddly he had a beat-up convertible with a door that fell off the hinge when you opened it and the window had to be pulled up manually. If I didn't have enough doubts about this guy already, he told me he lived in an apartment he shared and his room was next to the trash dumpster. He said he slept on an air mattress with a small hole so it had to be inflated every other day. While the pieces of his identity didn't fit, there was something about him I liked.

As time went on, we continued to see one another. He would usually fly to St. Louis because it was difficult for me to get away from my three businesses. Frankie, however, had a limousine transportation business with a driver on call. This is what allowed him to go back and forth at will.

Each time we were together, I felt like we shared some special moments but he would jokingly say, "My whole life is a lie." I would always try to gently pry but never really got any answers which were substantial; this disturbed me. He was telling me about his life being a lie yet there was something so sincere and honest about this guy; I couldn't resist wanting to spend more time with him.

What I did know is that he was accountable. Always. Whether we were miles and miles apart or if he was visiting me, he was always accessible and I could count on him to get things done. There was, however, one more paradox to his personality. He had no real commitments in his life yet he was so dependable and genuine. He was so simple, laid back and so removed from the world of business and stress that I almost found it refreshing. At least that's what I kept telling myself.

Although I was obviously very attracted to this handsome guy, that is the part of him that I mistrusted and liked the least. Men who have their looks to fall back on seldom seem to develop their personalities. Not Frankie. His personality was big. No one was a stranger to him. When we met, my professional life was fast and busy and everything in my life was rush, hurry, contemplate, analyze and produce. Then there was Frankie just floating along.

He was a bit mysterious because he looked happy and calm on the exterior even though he did not have a game plan for life. He would sound strong and together and then occasionally (during the first seven or eight months we were dating) he would throw in thoughts that sounded more confused. I felt like there were things he wanted me to know and was testing my reactions. I asked myself many times, "What are his hidden thoughts and secrets?"

The one thing I noticed is that every time we were together, he made me feel special. He made me feel like I was his priority and that he enjoyed seeing me happy. This was so totally different from my past relationships. And he did this on a consistent basis. He was so good looking and in such great shape that you would think that his life would be all about him. But it was completely the opposite. After our first meeting in Florida, he sent me a card that was so touching and genuine, I couldn't believe it. He was the most giving person I had ever been with.

I thought about my dad so often who is easy going and handles whatever comes his way; I always wished I could find someone like him, a Dick Van Dyke type of guy. Having been involved in one broken relationship after another, I was seriously beginning to doubt if I would ever meet my one true love. Then again there was something so uniquely invigorating about Frankie. I tried to repress the lingering questions in the back of my mind but it was to no avail.

Could he be that man? If so, were there any chinks in his armor?

~ ~ ~

Trusting Her Instincts

There was only one thing about Frankie that didn't sit well with me. He was a chain smoker. That was a huge chink in his armor. I mean the type who used one cigarette to light the next one. Here I was with a lung disease and he smoked. This was a dilemma I would soon have to address. Before addressing that particular one, however, I had to first see if Frankie passed the ultimate test – Mom and Dad.

I was naturally nervous about introducing Frankie to them. My mother had pointed out to me more than once that I had made some poor decisions in trusting my instincts with men. This was blatantly true. I wanted Frankie to make a good impression because I genuinely cared about him and wanted Mom and Dad to like him. Frankie, however, was not the least bit worried about making a good impression. There was nothing pretentious about him. He was going to be himself whether my parents approved or not.

So I planned a trip to Kansas City. I vividly remember the moment Mom opened the front door to greet us. I received a huge hug while Frankie received a fake air-hug. I could read Mom and Dad's faces so easily even though their reactions were warm and welcoming. Deep down they were thinking, "She did it again!"

Within the first hour of being home, Mom said we needed to go shopping for a few things and wondered what my guest would like to do while we were gone. (I knew Mom wanted to talk heart-to-heart to me alone.) Frankie spoke right up and said, "I'd be happy to go with you and give a male's opinion on clothing if you want one." What? Is there a man who actually wants to go shopping with women? I know this only made Mom more skeptical of his sincerity and motive. It didn't help either that he was so handsome. It just made things worse!

~ ~ ~

Felicia's First Impressions of Frankie

Dear Beth,

Friends and activities notwithstanding, Seymour and I knew a true companion was missing in Shelly's life. We were so pleased, however, where she was with her career and devotion to taking good care of herself that we focused on little else. Then just when we were beginning to think she had come to her senses as far as men were concerned, she and her girlfriend went on vacation to Ft. Lauderdale.

As we would soon discover, this vacation turned into far more than enjoying some time on the beach, touring the time-share location and returning home. When she called to tell me about meeting Frankie, my first thought was, "This guy is a real player who has rehearsed the same alluring words to Shelly that he's said to many other women." Then when she called to say that she had invited him to visit her in St. Louis, I thought, "What in the world is she thinking?"

Here was a muscle-bound guy with an East Coast accent who

didn't speak like we spoke and whose upbringing was so different from ours. He had no business of consequence and no ambition to do more. He did have a great sense of humor and was intelligent. The only other redeeming quality that was apparent was his nice hand-writing! He was a massage therapist which seemed a bit peculiar to us. Shelly had told us that although he lived a more liberal-seeming lifestyle, he had very conservative values. She said he was strictly against drugs, breaking laws and abided by moral rules.

If that weren't enough, his desire to walk on the beach and write poetry seemed even more peculiar. Although we liked him and appreciated his respect for us and for Shelly's incredible abilities, we couldn't imagine how this could be a budding, long-standing relationship. One thing, however, was abundantly clear. Shelly looked at him differently than any man she'd ever dated. It was also clear that he cared about her health. Seymour and I were left asking ourselves, "Could she be in love with him and was he the real deal?" It wouldn't be long until these questions were answered.

Fondly,
Felicia

~ ~ ~

The 'Eventful' Date

I was truthfully never bothered or concerned that Frankie didn't have a steady career, Beth. His lifestyle and lack of commitment didn't worry me whereas it would have with other men I'd dated. Frankie didn't need me to save him or change him like other men had. I just found him to be easy (no hassle and no fuss) and that seemed to work for me. I've always been self-sufficient and independent (some may say a little stubborn) so dating someone who did not judge, hinder, interfere or try to change me was comforting. While I felt safe with him, I'm certain my family and friends thought I had lost it!

On my third trip to visit Frankie, he had planned a trip to the Florida Keys; he loved the area and was visibly excited to take me there. He planned for me to fly into Ft. Lauderdale on Thursday night and Friday we would get up at 5 a.m. and head south to the Keys on a 4.5 hour drive. Right there I was already a little nervous; having a lung disease made flying risky (germs) and then staying up late and getting up early are usually not a healthy combination. I went with the plan because I didn't want to raise any red flags by making my health problems sound worse than they were.

During the middle of the night, I started getting very intense lung pains that mimicked the pleurisy pain I've had before where I don't even want to breathe. Plus I had a fever (I always travel with a thermometer) of about 101 degrees. All I could think about was lying in my own bed as opposed to the air mattress I was on and eating chicken soup versus the McDonalds breakfast sandwich and not doing anything until I felt better (versus driving 4.5 hours in a car with no air conditioner in 104 degree summer heat). But for some reason in the morning when we were ready to leave, the words "This is going to be fun" came out of my mouth and we were on our way.

I told Frankie that working out was my life-line and that I would need to find a gym and run on a treadmill at some point that day. So when we got to the Keys, we unpacked and headed out to the only gym in Key West. The good news was that they only charged $5 for a day pass; the bad news was that the treadmills were made out of refurbished boat wood and were probably put together back in the 60's. One treadmill out of four actually worked.

The gym, which was run by an older gentleman who was hard of hearing, also had a boxing ring. There was literally one light bulb which barely lit up the gym enough to see where you were walking. But I got on my treadmill and ran in spite of carrying a fever I hadn't mentioned to Frankie. At the end of the run I was so parched and dehydrated that I asked for some water.

When we looked in the case, there was one bottle of water left. Just one! Perfect! That's all I needed. Frankie took it out of the case and said to the man, "I'm laying down the money for the water here on your counter."

I took a big swig and set the bottle back down while I searched for a towel to wipe off. As we looked back at the counter, the man was gulping the last sip of water out of our bottle as he mumbled, "Looks like someone accidentally left a few dollars here" and put the money in his register. Things only got worse from there . . .

Frankie had planned for us to play golf because he knew I loved the game. He had reservations at a small 18-hole course which he decided we should walk for exercise. We played the entire 18 holes in 104 degrees of heat and then he said, "Do you want to play more?"

What? I couldn't breathe, I was hot, dehydrated and ready to pass out. So I suggested maybe we relax in a cool area. We literally fell asleep and woke up five hours later. I am certain we both had heat exhaustion. I finally had to tell him that I thought I had a little cold and didn't feel all that well. He was so attentive and sympathetic to my needs which revealed another glimpse of his caring nature. Although he had originally come across as someone who didn't care about anything, his actions said it all.

He suggested we go down to the ocean, take a dip and then go to a quaint romantic spot in the evening and watch the stars. This sounded good because it would take very little effort on my part. When we walked into the water, it was like walking into a dirty hot bathtub. The water temperature had to be close to 90 degrees and the sand felt like gushing mud. I tried to act like it was refreshing but it was hard to fake, so we retreated to the romantic and secluded patio area that looked out over the ocean and a beautiful starry sky.

As we settled into our lounge chairs, it suddenly felt like I was lying on a cactus. What were all these little needles poking me? I didn't say anything but it was now obvious that something was poking and pinching me everywhere! I could see Frankie squirming in his chair, too. Frankie looked at me finally and said, "Are you getting eaten alive by the "no-see-ums" microscopic little bugs that bite?"

Once we escaped the painful attack of insects, we cracked up laughing how our entire day was one miserable thing after the other and how much fun it was to be miserable together in the Keys. I was also feeling worse so we decided to head back to Ft. Lauderdale in the morning.

We headed home on a Sunday knowing there would be less traffic. After we got about 40 miles outside of the Keys, Frankie heard something slip in the engine and suddenly the car dropped into 1st gear reducing our speed to 20 mph. The car wouldn't budge out of that gear which meant we'd be traveling at the pitiful speed of 20 mph for the next 200 miles with no service stations open.

To get to know someone well, you need to see them at their lowest point. Now after our last few days, you would think this would be a dramatically low point for both of us. Instead we became hysterical. Then Frankie had a great idea. He was a gold member of AAA and they allow two tows per year that can't exceed 100 miles each. Perfect! We were approximately 203 miles from home, so we called a tow truck that hauled us 100 miles to Isla Morada where the car was dropped off at a motel where we slept that night. The next day we called another tow truck and they towed us exactly 100 miles which means they literally unloaded Frankie's car in the middle of Commercial Boulevard. We then drove the remaining 2.5 miles down the street with flashers on and cars honking at us in disgust for cruising along at a blazing speed of 20 mph.

What is so interesting to me looking back is that I owned a nice home, a 2 bed/2 bath condo, three salons and spas and drove a beautiful Saab. Yet here I was with lung pain and a fever having more fun in a broken down LeBaron with a guy who I am not sure had a real job. I liked this care-free character more and more. In fact, I loved being with him more and more. A few days later I flew back to St. Louis and was admitted to the hospital with pneumonia. I don't remember if I even told Frankie I was there. I was completely consumed with getting better so I could be with him again as soon as possible.

~ ~ ~

Let's be 'Frank'

I clearly remember the day Frankie and I finally had a very candid conversation about our personal lives, all skeletons in our closets and our feelings on the future. At this point we had been dating about a year. He visited me in St. Louis and the only reason he wanted to go back to Florida was the weather. He never seemed to feel an urgency to get back to his job. I found that somewhat confusing because I was now 43 years old and well into my career. I figured he surely had to have some kind of plan for his life. Yet he never talked about it.

I brought up the conversation based on a phrase he often repeated: "My whole life is a lie." I felt like it was time for him to come clean and explain what he meant. I figured I would trade him information. I told him that I, too, had not told him everything and that we each needed to bare our souls if we were to continue dating. He confessed that he had grown up quite poor, had little parental direction, had no future plans and that his work which was very sporadic couldn't sustain him financially. He told me about his past, his relationships (if you want to call them that) and his family life that was completely different than mine.

He didn't seem embarrassed or ashamed; it was just very matter of fact. I think he was waiting for me to react but I was silent. I didn't know what to think. I didn't know if I was happy he had told me the truth about his entire life or if I was more puzzled by his complete lack of a plan. He said he'd always done odds-and-ends work on his own because one day he wanted to have his own business; he said he wasn't the type to work for someone else. I related to that.

Now it was my turn. I told him I had cystic fibrosis and that it was a progressive lung disease. I said I was fortunate because other than the times I got really sick and had to be hospitalized, I was pretty healthy. I think he asked a few questions; I know he appreciated hearing about my CF because he'd wondered why I coughed so much. With CF, it is common to have interrupted sleep each night due to trouble breathing and uncontrollable coughing from lung congestion.

That was the extent of our conversation about my disease. The only other thing I mentioned is that cigarettes were very damaging to my health and this would be an issue if we continued dating. He remarked that he was very conscious never to smoke inside or while standing next to me which was true. Then he spontaneously said, "Maybe I will just quit." I didn't want to seem overly anxious and excited because I knew that people who smoked the way he did could quit many times over with little or no success. I didn't say much and we left it at that.

You know that point in a relationship where you really like someone and you are sure they really like you but the word 'love' has never been mentioned? Even more trivial was the fact that we'd never discussed dating one another exclusively; so nothing about a long-term relationship could be presumed. There were too many uncertainties.

A few weeks later when Frankie was back in Florida, I heard an ad on talk radio about a female hypnotist in St. Louis who specialized in helping people lose weight and quit smoking with guaranteed results. Didn't they all? But I called her and she told me she had a successful track record; she also said you pay once and you never have to pay again. I gave my credit card information and told her my boyfriend would come see her when he returned to St. Louis.

When Frankie arrived a few weeks later, I told him about the hypnotist. He said he was someone who could not be hypnotized but if it meant a lot to me he would try it. Fair enough. He went to the appointment and called me one hour later.

I said, "How did it go?"

"Sorry to tell you but I think you just threw away $90. What a crock! I was awake the whole time and I don't feel any differently."

"So what do we do now?"

He said she mentioned that when he saw the color 'red' it would remind him not to smoke. Although I was a little disheartened to hear his news, I felt good that he at least made an attempt. For the heck of it, I hung a red tank top on the lamp in the corner of my apartment and a red pair of shorts on the kitchen chandelier. When we returned to my apartment later that day, he said he wanted a cigarette but hadn't smoked one yet. He also said, "I can't promise you I won't smoke again because I still have the urge. I just won't have one yet."

That was 11 years ago. He never touched a cigarette again. His strong resolve and commitment to change validated what my heart and soul had been telling me for months.

I was with someone who cared deeply for me.

~ ~ ~

Mission Accomplished

It was now early in 2003 and Frankie and I had been dating long distance with him spending more time in Missouri. We were in search of finding a way for him to stay busy and productive. I said I'd like to develop a skin care product or body product we could sell in my salons. Frankie, meanwhile, had just read a book on making millions through mail orders. We agreed we could come up with a successful idea but weren't sure what it would be.

Because of the treatments and medications I had to take with my disease, my skin was always dry; I had also lost some elasticity in my face and body after losing a lot of weight. I told him there were so many women in our spas who had these same issues and maybe this would be a good place to start. I spent the next several months learning about ingredients, treatments, the anatomy of skin and formulations that would evolve into creating a good skin care product.

While I did this, Frankie continued reading books about the mail order business and learned it was a numbers game; one book guaranteed you could make millions if you mailed flyers to thousands of people. This sounded good. Now we needed the product.

A few weeks later I found a type of aloe vera that was the only medical grade of aloe used by large companies like Johnson & Johnson to help repair skin on burn victims. This type of aloe was being harvested in another country then processed and sold in Dallas. The studies on it were so intriguing; I wondered if it could repair skin that had been stretched and marked from the loss of elasticity. We provided a body service in our spas that helped women lose inches but there was no type of take-home product to use as maintenance between treatments. I thought it would be wonderful to have something like this for the customers to maintain healthy skin.

At the same time, I also researched hundreds of ingredients and found data on another ingredient that looked like a perfect companion to the aloe. It was also natural and was a protein found in the ice glaciers of Antarctica. Don't ask what possessed me but I told Frankie we had to fly to Dallas and learn about this aloe. I was determined to see if we could make a deal with this company to invent a body product from their aloe along with this other added protein.

Frankie was totally on board. (Of course, I would have to pay for the trip and lodging as his funds were meager.) I had a vision and was on a mission. Frankie came up with a name he thought would be ideal for a company that made natural products by combining two ingredients that worked together. He suggested we call our new venture 'NatureSynergy.'

I loved it!

Long story endless . . . we went to Dallas. We toured the plant and sat with the head of operations. With a big promise of growth on our end, they agreed to let us work with their in-house chemist and formulate our dream product that would hydrate, help with stretch marks and cellulite and firm the skin. They even agreed to work with us on payment terms and inventory stock. I don't know if our timing was just right or if they saw the dream in our eyes but three months later our first product called 'Hydratone' was launched.

Now we had to sell it. I knew it would not be difficult to sell in my salons because we already had a customer base of people who were getting services and trusted me. However, we needed to move a lot more than that if we were to ever get through the first run of 3,000 units. With Frankie's fool-proof mail order plan in place, he was now moving into high gear. He had an entire set-up with a mailing list we purchased, a color flyer we printed of the 'before and after pictures' we took in our spas and a money back guarantee.

At the same time we developed this product, a vendor visited my salon with a product that was a salt scrub made from essential oils. It was fantastic to the touch and smell and once you rubbed this concoction on your hands and feet and rinsed it off, your skin felt like butter.

However, it was expensive considering it was sea salt in a bunch of oils. Now I was in full chemist mode and thought why not develop our own product like it and have a two-step offer in our spas and mail orders. I called the lab that was making our body product and they told me about a lab they worked with in Dallas that could perhaps help us with this product since they usually only produced aloe products. They could only do our Hydratone. We contacted the lab and explained what we wanted and after many conversations and prototypes, we launched 'Sea Spa.' Now we had two products that could be used together and we could sell this system in our spas, on radio ads and at local trade shows.

Frankie spent day after day sending out flyers from the mailing list. He'd read if something was addressed by hand it had a 50% better chance of being opened. So he hand-addressed hundreds of envelopes daily. I think we got two orders. Now we had thousands of bottles of Hydratone and 5000 jars of Sea Spa and were barely selling any of them outside of our spas. Since we had two body products, I thought it only made sense to have some facial skin care products to go with them; I thought skin care may be easier to sell. I was really into research and formulas at this point. In fact, I was virtually obsessed with learning as much as I could about ingredients and thinking of ways to market our products.

Linda had a friend who used a lab in St. Louis to make tanning products and she introduced me to the owners of Westport Labs who then introduced me to their lead chemist. Everyone liked the idea of working with us to formulate our own line of skin care. They were a large fragrance lab but didn't produce much in the way of skin care and liked the idea of this new direction.

Months and months later, thousands of dollars later and thousands of hours lost in sleep, we developed a new 5-piece line of skin care. We had our special aloe and glacial protein ingredients as the main components and we had a great marketing story developed. Now we had to get out and sell it or we would go broke trying to pay off our debts from this risky business venture.

We initially decided to do home-spa parties for women. I could have the manicure gal from my salon do paraffin hand treatments, my massage therapist do chair massages and Frankie and I could do facials on the guests with our new line of skin care. Of course, my mother stepped right up to the plate and started asking and begging her best friends and our relatives to have home parties. In all honesty, everyone said "Yes" out of love. No one likes to do these but Mom got us booked with four parties in Kansas City and my sister, Lori, arranged for two more. It was a lot of work but we were making money and honing our skills at selling our new product line.

From 2002-2003, my health was basically stable. I still did my usual daily treatments and at that time I only had to be hospitalized once within the year. Our lives were sedate for the most part. Frankie was not interested in staying out late at night which enabled me to stay healthier.

At this point, I still didn't want him to know or worry too much about my disease. I guess I didn't want him to think it would interfere with our lives, so when I made my hospital visit to "clean out" my lungs when he was back in Florida, I didn't tell him. I simply went to the hospital for a few days and did my home IV's for another seven days and he never knew. Looking back, I think how silly it was to hide this from him. He'd already shown his kind and caring soul in so many ways and I know he would have wanted to help me.

~ ~ ~

The Final Farewell

It was now well into 2003 and Frankie and I were really enjoying all the time we spent together and both of us hated the times we were apart. He was getting tired of being away from the beauty of the Florida beaches he loved so much while I led a busy life with my businesses in St. Louis. We now had our own start-up business together and although it was maybe only generating $100 a month, we both felt committed to the success of 'Nature Synergy.'

I was getting more and more agitated every time we'd talk on the phone and he would say, "Just another day in paradise." If I heard that expression one more time, I would scream! He always sounded so carefree and content. When he was back in Florida, it made me wonder all over again if he was right for me. How could someone be so happy by living life one day at a time?

Soon thereafter, a prominent plastic surgeon in St. Louis approached me about opening a large medi-spa that would serve as his surgery center but also have a full upscale spa. This would be something that no one else was doing in St. Louis at the time; it would also require a very sizeable investment. He wanted me to be his partner. I loved the idea and was ready for a new challenge as our three 'Beauty Source' locations were doing well. I decided it would be a good idea for me to work at his current location first to get a feel for that type of environment.

So I worked a few hours a week and on weekends answering phones, booking the appointments and filing records. There were no windows in my office and I had a 30-minute break for lunch. I was also embedded with office workers who gossiped about one another which was totally depressing.

I made a spontaneous trip to Florida to get away from things. It was picturesque the day my plane landed opposed to the cold and lonely days in St. Louis. The weekend together was wonderful and I dreaded returning home. As Frankie and I were sitting on the wall that extends down the entire three-mile stretch of Ft. Lauderdale beach, the sun was setting and we could feel the warm breeze sweeping across our faces. I had to leave for the airport in an hour as we clung to those last few tender moments together. The time spent with him was precious and Florida was starting to feel like home. As he held me in his arms, our eyes exchanged endearing tears and he said, "You can have this every day."

"Frankie, I can't. I have a life, friends, family and businesses I can't leave behind."

I felt a twinge of anger at how simple he made it sound. As I got out of the car at the airport and we hugged goodbye, he said, "Shelly, you know as well as anyone that life is short. If you want something bad enough, you have to make it happen."

As I boarded the plane, I was overwhelmed by a rush of emotions. I cried for almost an hour. I don't know if I was sad or scared. Sad that I knew we could not continue dating long distance or scared that I had to make a move. There was one thing I knew for certain. I was not ready to say farewell to someone who now meant so much to me. Instead it was time to say farewell to my home and friends. It was time to move to Florida.

~ ~ ~

Truth and Consequences

When I landed in St. Louis and walked out of the airport, I looked around and felt like a visitor. Was it possible that during a four-hour plane ride I divorced myself from my life here? Or was it possible that I had emotionally begun detaching myself months ago? All I could focus on is what I would say to Linda and Dale, to my salon employees who had become friends and to my close girlfriends. It was even harder to think about moving further away from my family.

There was always comfort in knowing my parents and sisters were only a three-and-a-half hour drive from my home. Yet my mind was made up. I suppose the same type of strong will I have in life and in business also carried over to my personal life. Once my mind is made up, I really never look back.

A part of me was invigorated, excited and ready for a new challenge. While some people fear change, I embrace it. I was ready to take that leap of faith, move to a new city and relinquish my heart to someone I knew was my soul mate forever. Another part of me thought, "This is absolutely crazy!" I had no business plan, no job, nowhere to live, no doctor and a boyfriend who had even less than that. I was left with only two certainties: faith in myself and a sizeable savings.

I knew Mom and Dad and my sisters would have very mixed emotions. As a close-knit family, though, we have always wanted what is best for each other. They knew how hard the cold weather was on my health and I think that was one of the primary reasons they were supportive of my decision. Although they never said anything, I'm sure they had to be wondering if I was giving up everything for someone who promised me no long-term commitment or plan. There was no guarantee in their minds that Frankie could or would take care of me.

One thing Mom was adamant about was locating an adult CF clinic before I made any plans to move. She insisted that my next trip to Florida include an introduction and appointment with a new CF doctor in the area. My doctors in St. Louis told me about a clinic in West Palm. They knew of excellent doctors there who could monitor my health issues and scheduled a time for me to meet with them during my next trip to Florida.

I don't remember exactly how I told Linda that I would be moving. I can't believe I ever had the courage. She and the salons had been my life for nearly 10 years. Once I shared my plans with her, she and I agreed that we could not tell any of our 100+ employees. She didn't have an interest in keeping the salons and running the business herself so we agreed it would be best to sell all three beauty salons.

Because our salons were so successful, we knew it wouldn't take long to sell the three locations. Ideally we wanted to find one buyer to take all three but due to the size of the investment it would take to buy them, we knew they might need to be divided. We used a business broker who originally helped me when I bought my first Mail Boxes Etc. store so I knew he was trustworthy and a fast worker. Within a few months, we had a very interested buyer in our 'Beauty Source 1' location. After a few months of meetings, negotiations, auditing of our books and many legal contracts, we finally had a deal that Linda and I were very happy with overall.

During this period, many of the employees started sensing something was happening and in the process we lost a few employees. Once the deal was signed, we had a company meeting and explained that it was time for me to be with Frankie and that we both wanted to grow our new NatureSynergy company. I was always closest to the girls in my first salon since that is where I started. They were like family and when they first met Frankie, they were very skeptical. This is another instance where his good looks worked against him. Most doubted his sincerity and motives. As time went on and they got to know him, they saw a caring guy with a huge heart. Although they were happy for me, they were understandably worried about their futures.

Panic spread once word got out among our three locations. One of our head stylists met with us and asked if she and her husband could buy our second location where she worked. It was the smallest of all three and she was a smart stylist with good business sense. All the people in the shop liked and respected her so we knew this would be in all of their best interests. This was easy and now things were moving quickly.

In the meantime, I also had a condo to sell. Only seven months prior to all this, I felt like I was ready for my own place. I was tired of living in an apartment and had no inkling of leaving St. Louis, so I bought a condo within a mile of my primary salon location. Now I needed to sell it. A friend of Linda's had been looking to buy a house and was very interested. We quickly made a deal which left me a little behind in what I had invested in fixing it up but the trade-off of not having to put it on the market and finding an agent was worth it.

Now we needed to sell 'Beauty Source 3' and our mega-tanning salon called 'Sun Source.' Our broker found a gal who was in advertising and thought it would be glamorous to own a salon. She had the interest and plenty of funds so this was an easy and fast transaction. During the process of this sale, we lost about seven stylists who were afraid of the change and left. However, we had over 45 employees at that location so it didn't leave the salon even close to empty and we had a waiting list of stylists who wanted to work there.

I've always said, "Follow through with something until it doesn't make sense." This was all making sense so I knew I was doing the right thing. This didn't make it any easier, though, to say goodbye to so many dear friends. I will always cherish this letter I received from Tomasa, one of my employees. Her sentiments are a reminder of the close connections I'd made.

Dear Shelly,

I will never forget how we met in December of 2000. You walked into the restaurant where I was bussing tables. You tried to help me clean the table and I told you it was my job. You then told my husband, who also worked at the restaurant, what a hard worker I was. When you told him you owned a hair salon, he smiled and said that had been my career in my country.

You said, "It's too bad Tomasa doesn't speak English because I would love to have an employee like her."

You then intuitively introduced yourself and told me about your business. You knew some Spanish words and I knew very little English. Somehow we understood each other and you insisted that I was wasting my talents. You were determined to figure out a way to get me into your salon with my limited English.

My husband took me to the salon for my first day to assist the stylists with their needs as well as do the laundry. I noticed that no one spoke to me in Spanish. I felt lost and bored so I started cleaning the whole salon. I didn't want to go back after that first day. You insisted that I come back and give it one more try so I did. I'm not sure what you said but everyone started to speak what Spanish words they knew and it made me feel the opposite of what I felt that first day.

I went to school to get my cosmetology license because mine from Mexico wasn't accepted in the United States. You gave me the opportunity to go to school and work for you. While giving me more responsibilities, you pushed me to learn more and be successful in the business.

You never told me about your disease. You were always happy and worked hard. A few years later you weren't in the shop and I asked the stylists where you were. They said you were in the hospital and I asked what happened. When I learned you had cystic fibrosis, I realized more than ever how strong you are because you never complained about feeling sick. You inspired me to push myself more.

I now have my own business because of you. If we hadn't met, I wouldn't be the ambitious person I am today; you gave me confidence in myself. Whenever I was afraid to try a new task you asked me to do, you said, "Tomasa, I wouldn't ask if I thought you couldn't do it."

I will miss you when you move to Florida but we will always be good friends and will talk often. I will always ask for your advice because you will always be my mentor. Even with your busy schedule you will find time for me.

I love you, Shelly! Thank you for being in my life.

Tomasa

Shelly (second from left) age 6

Shelly (background left) playing softball

1975

The sisters
From left: Mindy, Shelly and Lori

Felicia and Seymour

Shelly on the treadmill

Breathing treatment and IV PICC line

Frankie's card to Shelly

Shelley, 4-23-01

Thank You For Giving me A LifeTime of happiness in one short week.

Even Though we will be many miles APART, You will be Close To me in heart & Soul.

I will be in ST Louis To See You Soon!

Love Always
Frankie

Shelly and Frankie's Wedding

Shelly with Carrie Ann Inaba of Dancing with the Stars

Shelly with her models backstage at H.S.N. From left, Beverly, Ingerborg, Shelly and Kara

Shelly demonstrating her 2-minute miracle exfoliating face gel on HSN

Shelly and Frankie 2011

Shelly as a skin care developer and radiant spokeswoman on HSN

~ ~ ~

Time to Meet Frankie

Dear Beth,

The next email you receive won't be from me. It will be from Frankie. I'm anxious for you to meet the man I love so dearly and deeply. I can't continue to tell my story from this point forward without him. He has been my partner and my heart and soul for eleven years.

Shelly

~ ~ ~

My Shelly

Hi Beth.

I've enjoyed watching Shelly's excitement as you've been working together to tell her life story. I've been looking forward to this opportunity to express my love for this beautiful woman.

I really am the luckiest man in the world. The best day of my life was meeting her at that red light in Ft. Lauderdale. Eleven years later we are still crazy in love with one another and have a successful business together. But most importantly, today is a great day for Shelly and her health. She feels good today and I am thankful for every day that I am blessed with her presence.

Shelly is someone who actually uses her cystic fibrosis condition as a training ground for her successes in life. She challenges herself to fight her disease by living each day with this belief:

"If I feel good today (she has these days once in a while) then I can feel good tomorrow." That's what inspires her to run each day, eat the right foods, take all her meds and do her breathing treatments. You'll never meet a more courageous person in your life.

I can't imagine being told at 12 years of age that I may not live past my 18th birthday. Shelly's response to this was "NO WAY!" She is now 51 years old, has a thriving business, has made me a better man and is an inspiration to everyone in our community. You will be amazed by her will to live; you will be even more amazed by her positive personality and what she has accomplished. She is a role model for CF patients because she is dedicated to 'living life.' Shelly represents hope. She makes her disease an inconvenience, not a death sentence.

I have been saying for so long that she should write a book. This could not only help CF patients but the masses as well. Her story will inspire so many to be proactive and reach for their dreams regardless of the circumstances. I see her book being on shelves all across America. Thank you for making my dream come true. I want to share my Shelly with the world.

I'll send another email tomorrow morning. You need to know how she saved my life.

Frankie

~ ~ ~

Finding His Purpose

I was always a carefree guy from Rhode Island who never worried about tomorrow. My existence consisted of living with my mother most of my life until I was 34 years old. I did this for two reasons: it was cheaper than getting my own place and I needed to take care of her.

My social life was pretty much spent taking advantage of a string of women who I would meet, maybe take out once or twice and never call again. I had this act down to a smooth routine. I was very good at it because I was blessed with good looks and a physically fit body that women found attractive. Unfortunately I abused this blessing by being a jerk. Do I feel badly about it now? That is a big "Yes" but I can't change the past. I was a guy with no credible work history and never stayed at a job long because I had no special skills, no college degree and no ambition. I quit more than a dozen jobs along the way.

One day my buddy and I decided we'd rent a U-Haul truck and move to Florida. By now I was 36 years old and my focus was on sunshine, the ocean and being with women who would spend money on me and basically support me. Talk about a shallow life that was going nowhere. I never worried about my future and what it would be like with no savings and no career.

The beginning of my lucky break was the day I met Shelly. I had crossed that street hundreds of times and never once looked at the car passengers stopped at the red light. I sometimes wonder why she pulled over to meet me when I was a stranger. I wonder why I was blessed that day? Why did God put me in that moment of time? Today I know the answer. God wanted to save my life and in the process give me a purpose. That purpose was to take care of Shelly with her disease.

She was my gift from God and my purpose for living. She made me a better man who walked away from womanizing, unethical behavior and laziness. Because of Shelly, I have found beauty in life and joy in the extreme commitment it has taken for me to be a good person.

Shelly changed me as I watched her suffer with her disease and yet remain such a kind and genuine human being. She taught me that I didn't have to lift weights and use my masculine charm to deceive people. I didn't have to fake my life anymore.

~ ~ ~

The Defining Moment

Shelly told me she had cystic fibrosis on our second date. I really didn't have much of a reaction because I knew this was only going to be a short-term relationship. I didn't know there was any other kind. I had decided years ago that I would never commit to being with one woman my whole life.

Before I knew it, we had been together two years. In the back of my mind, I thought maybe we'd last a few more years and our business venture would fail like every other job I had. Sure I liked Shelly. I couldn't help but like this beautiful, sweet woman.

In those two years we were together, she had to be hospitalized different times. I was always right by her side. By now she was 42 and had already lived far beyond her life expectancy. Then the unexpected happened that I never saw coming.

We were at the hospital waiting for some test results that could have been a death sentence for her. Shelly started crying as I held her in my arms. I felt so sorry for her because I knew her tears were pure fear for her life ending far too soon. I was wrong. Her tears were for me. She looked up and said, "Who is going to take care of you, Frankie, if something happens to me?"

Are you kidding me? Did she just say what I thought she said? I've only known her a short time and she cares about me this much? Her life is at stake and she's worried about my future? I knew at that moment for the first time in my shallow life that I finally wanted to marry a woman and fly straight. I knew for the first time in my life what it felt like to love someone. This moment gave me a second chance at life; I would be with a woman who truly cared for me unconditionally. I had found my soul mate, a woman I vowed to love and take care of forever. Shelly saved me.

~ ~ ~

Serendipity

Beth, I just read the emails Frankie sent you. Let me share my intimate recollection of the day I was at the stoplight when we made eye contact. The word 'serendipity' comes to mind because it was a fortunate discovery for both of us that happened by accident. Now I have to ask myself if it really was an accident that I met him. I believe in the power of the Lord and I have to think He planned for us to meet that day. There is no other reason that explains the critical moment in time when a mere 60 seconds in the car at a stoplight could change my future in such a dramatic and positive way.

Before I continue with the next roller coaster of events that Frankie and I experienced in building our company, I want to add these thoughts in response to your asking me the other day if I feared death and if I prayed.

I Talk ... God Listens

I was on the treadmill at the gym yesterday doing my usual daily run. I also did my usual coughing and those who know me ignored it. I often joke with these friends that one day I will be lying on the ground dying and gasping for air and they will walk right over me since they are so used to hearing the sound of my coughing and choking when I run. However, when new people are running next to me for the first time, I always explain that I don't have a cold but rather a lung disease. I don't want them to think they can catch what I have. Many look at me with a blank expression. Some say, "I am so sorry" and there was one gal who broke down in tears. When I asked her if she knew someone who had CF, she said, "No, I don't really know what it is but it sounds so painful." I had to console her so that she could get back to running.

This morning, however, I told the gal next to me about having CF and she said her best friend's daughter in Illinois also has the disease. She's in college and is very sick right now. The way they were dealing with her CF (or not dealing with it) was tearing the family apart. I told her about my teens and growing up with it and how my views have changed as an adult. I also said I would pray for her friend and her daughter's health.

I then said a little prayer to God as I was running. I talk to Him all the time and I know He listens. I actually think He listens to me so intently that I'm careful not to ask for much because I don't want Him to feel like it's His job to "fix" me. I don't ever want to seem ungrateful or spoiled because none of us are promised a life of ease and happiness at all times. My prayers are nearly always centered on thanking Him for what he does for me, my family, friends and loved ones.

This time when I thanked Him, I said how good I was feeling today. I don't have that many days anymore when I feel great and when I do, it DOES NOT go unrecognized or unappreciated.

As I looked out the oversized picture window at the fitness center and stared at the tall, strong palm trees and vibrant blue sky, I thanked God for giving me the strength to run; I prayed that He will continue to watch over my family and Frankie's family who are so close to our hearts. I thank Him daily for keeping Frankie healthy and giving me the gift of someone I treasure, value and love more and more every day of my life.

Then I said, "I wish I could meet you." But right after I said that I hoped He didn't think I meant right now. What if He thought that was His signal that I was ready for heaven?

So I did what I do all the time. I amended and clarified my prayer. I explained that I look forward to meeting Him one day when the time was right and hopefully that wouldn't be for many many years. I was also hoping He didn't get a "call" from someone else praying at that moment and missed hearing my amended request.

You would think that when you have a life-threatening disease you would fear dying. Maybe some do but I don't. What I fear and think about almost daily (now that I am older and not as healthy) is what my passing would do to my parents and how it would affect their lives. I know their hearts would be shredded. I wouldn't be able to forgive myself for the hurt I would cause them. Who would call Mom to interrupt her daily activities with life-altering questions like, "Is my hair too light or too dark?" Who would laugh at my dad's jokes and repeat them to everyone else in case they didn't hear him? I also think about my sisters being sad at my funeral. I know they would be laughing and crying at the same time because we have a bad habit of laughing even in the face of crisis.

I think about Frankie a lot and picture him working in our office alone and sitting in his Archie Bunker over-sized recliner alone. I think about him going to lunch in his convertible without me. This saddens me so much that I can barely handle the thought.

There are times when I almost secretly hope he doesn't love me too much so that if I'm gone, the pain will not be unbearable. I tell him all the time that when I die one day, I want him to be sad for a month or so and then get out and meet a wonderful woman who loves him. That's when he flicks my nose and says, "Get out of here. You are crazy!" I know that he loves me and there is not anyone in the world who has shown me that more than Frankie (except Mom and Dad, of course) but once I am gone, I am gone. All I care about is his happiness.

Sometimes I ask God to let me outlive everyone I love and care about so deeply. Then I go back, as I always do, and clarify that; I ask to live an exceptionally long time rather than lose those I love. I also ask for a signal or some kind of warning prior to dying. I don't want to die and never know it. I want a "phase-in" period so I can get everything in order and say, "Thank you" to everyone I know and love. I find comfort in knowing that when I talk . . . God listens.

~ ~ ~

Paying Our Dues

The thought of moving to Florida felt like I was moving to another country. It was almost better that I didn't spend much time analyzing my decision or I might have deemed it insane. I had no plan except to get there and figure out a plan. We had promised the new salon owner of 'Beauty Source 1' that we would stay on for one month and help him through the transition. This was very stressful because the employees were hurt and many took it personally. Deep down inside it was really hard for me to think about saying goodbye to many of the people who had done so much for me over the years while we were growing.

Frankie flew to St. Louis and we hired a moving company to transport all my belongings. You don't realize how many pairs of black pants you own or how many times you bought the same spices until you have to move. As sad as I was to be leaving, I was equally excited about the future. We found a two-bedroom apartment in Del Ray Beach and thought it would be a good area to live. There was a fitness center right down the street, my new doctor's office was nearby in West Palm and the downtown beach area was only a 15-minute ride from our place.

We both were now officially unemployed and living off savings. We were forced to live as cheaply as possible; to bring in some extra money, we rented one of the bedrooms to Frankie's friend.

We continued working on the plan to market and grow our NatureSynergy company. We were confident that if we could get our products into the hands of women one-on-one, they would sell. We had two star products out of the six we now carried in our line. One was the Sea Spa because it was something that could be demonstrated on the hands which instantly made them look and feel 10 years younger. We also had a new emerging star product called the 2 Minute Miracle Gel. This product was amazing and ideal to demonstrate live because it is a gel which turns into a liquid; as you rub it, you actually see little balls of dead skin rolling up and forming on your face or wherever applied. Women were literally shocked when they saw how effectively it worked. The key was how to reach as many women as possible.

Frankie learned that in trade show marketing, it is a good idea to go where you won't have competition. We started looking at the schedules of craft fairs, trade shows, industrial shows, boat shows, bridal fairs, bowling shows and nursing association shows. At bowling shows we touted the need to get rid of calloused hands with our Sea Spa product. At nursing shows we demonstrated how doctors and nurses could get skin relief from their dry hands that were washed repeatedly. At boat shows we emphasized the benefits of taking care of dry and aging skin from sun exposure. We had a credible pitch for every venue.

We realized there were opportunities every week and weekend if we were willing to travel the state of Florida, put up a tent and table and stand around each day and sell. When we looked at the number of attendees at some of these events, we saw that many would draw close to 100,000 visitors. We were sure we'd hit a gold mine and that soon we would be selling hundreds of thousands of our products. We eventually learned that just because there were thousands of attendees, the two of us could only physically talk with a handful of ladies in an hour. There were many trade show events where we would work two 12-hour days and only sell 50 units.

We also found a 'green market' which was held in a beautiful park every Saturday and Sunday from 7 a.m.-2 p.m. that featured natural foods and produce. Since we carried a line of products created from aloe vera, they bent the rules and let us have a booth each week. This eventually became Frankie's worst nightmare every weekend once we realized we were spending $60 each week to make $20. He hated doing the green markets because it was frustrating knowing we had great products to sell and didn't have the money to advertise in a big way.

One particular morning it was rainy and windy. Our tent kept blowing over and our feet were submerged in puddles of rain. No one was coming to the green market that day and we still had three more hours to go. The rules stipulated that you had to stay unless they closed the market.

Frankie was whining repeatedly and begging me to leave early. He was relentless until I finally had no choice but to agree. He told me to use my CF as an excuse and tell the head chief that I was catching a cold and with my lungs it would be best if we could get approval to leave early.

Rudy, the man in charge, was so compassionate and kind and said, "Of course, you poor dear. You have my permission to go." I went back to tell Frankie the good news and right behind me was Rudy extending his hand to Frankie in a gesture to say, "Good man for taking care of her." When Rudy told Frankie he totally understood our need to leave early, Frankie said, "Well, I would stay but Shelly really feels like we should leave." Then Frankie turned to me and said, "Shelly, do you think you can make it another few hours? I hate to break the rules and leave early."

My eyes nearly bulged out of my head as I tried to disguise the

"I am going to strangle you" frustration I was feeling. Instead I said, "Of course, I can stick it out and stay." Frankie had thrown me under the bus because he was too chicken to stand up to Rudy. He felt too guilty. It has become our private joke to this day; when someone says one thing but does another, they have "Rudied you."

~ ~ ~

In Need of a Break

What seemed strange and at first very unsettling to me is that we had a more relaxed schedule. We were working hard but there were no set hours. We didn't even have an office and were sharing one old, slow computer. We went to the beach when we had time, worked out every day and had a much simpler life. Part of me felt guilty for not being more stressed out and instead enjoying the sunshine and beautiful surroundings every day.

The one thing I did constantly worry about was money. I had a nice bankroll saved when I moved but as time passed, we were spending more money than we were making and eventually our savings would be depleted. Of course, I didn't want to ever worry Mom and Dad so I would only report our successes to them. I told them about the money we were making at the trade shows and fairs and about the progress we were making in our home party division. We hadn't lost focus of our initial plan which was growing our home spa party division. However, moving to a new state and knowing very few people who would have a home party for us proved to be a huge challenge.

A few months after we moved, we received an email from a lady in Australia. She had used our products, loved them and wanted to sell them in her life-coaching business. She worked with massage therapists and estheticians and showed them how to expand their services. Her program was very successful and she found that these individuals were starved for new ways to make more money outside of the traditional spas. We realized this might be the key to our growth as well. Perhaps we could market a home spa party program to massage therapists and estheticians who wanted to have spa parties and sell products along with their services.

Having owned spas, I knew this idea wouldn't appeal to the traditional salons and spas because it would be taking business away from their locations. However, after being in the industry and reading the trade publications, we knew there were abundant numbers of massage therapists who had their own small businesses and didn't work out of a spa location. These were the people we had to reach.

Since Frankie had once been a licensed therapist, he knew there was a Massage Therapy Association which governed all licensed massage therapists nationwide. They also had hundreds of chapters throughout the country in every city. The chapters had their own trade shows and conventions throughout the year and there was a huge national trade show for the entire association once a year.

There were over 30 chapters in Florida and dozens and dozens of massage therapy schools throughout the state. If we could capture this market, we knew we could be successful but we needed a strong plan and money. It would be expensive to travel to these various locations; we also needed to develop marketing materials. We decided we had no other choice but to commit whatever money we had left to make this work.

~ ~ ~

PICC Problems

During this first year in Florida, I was keeping up with my health regimen; however, I still had my usual bouts of pneumonia. When oral antibiotics didn't work during one of these spells, I had to be admitted to a hospital. It was such a strange feeling to be in a new hospital in a new city with a new doctor and nursing staff. When you have CF, you are hospitalized so many times over the course of your life that you get to know all the staff on your hospital floor. The nurses, physical and occupational therapists, dietitians, doctors, interns and even many of the patients are familiar. For the first time in my life, however, I felt like I was completely taken care of because Frankie was with me every moment.

He hovered over me continually. Maybe subconsciously he felt like it was his duty to take good care of me since I moved to Florida to be with him. Maybe he felt a sense of responsibility. When I didn't feel well, he followed me around, occasionally putting his hand on my head to check for a temperature.

During my first hospitalization in Florida, I allowed him to drive me to the hospital and check me in but then he had to leave. He could visit a few times but only for a short period. I don't like visitors and I don't want even those I love most to see me this way. I don't want the attention to be focused on my being sick.

As my health has taken a steeper decline in recent years, I realize how much he truly wants to be with me every second in the hospital. I didn't realize earlier how much being by my side at all times meant to him. Now I need him there; he is my strength. When I hear him coming down the hall and he does 'our whistle' I light up knowing he is nearby.

The hospital is located in a very dangerous, rough part of town. It is a trauma center and there are helicopters continually bringing in patients with gunshot wounds all day and night. You can hear the voices announcing over the loud speaker "Trauma by air" which means the police and emergency staff need to stand by and be prepared. This is my cue every time. I slip on my tennis shoes, grab my IV pole and scurry out the front door, down the long, bumpy sidewalk and try to get to the emergency room entrance to greet the trauma team. It is all so interesting to me; I like to probe and find out as much as I can. It is usually something so awful and removed from anything I can imagine in my life that I find it totally intriguing. Although Frankie hates it when I do this because he worries about the surroundings and my safety, it satisfies my hidden desire to be in the forensics field.

During one unforgettable stay in the hospital, the aide took me to the radiology department to have the PICC line inserted. At that time, the radiologists used ultrasound to find the best vein placement for the line; this also allowed them more certainty that the line was properly placed in order to try and prevent my throwing a blood clot or dislodging the line.

After all the scrubbing and twenty minutes of prep work was done this particular day, the radiologist began the procedure. He gave me a shot to numb my arm and made the usual short cut in the skin and began threading the tube through my vein. As he got to my shoulder area, he met resistance. I started to sweat from the pressure when he began poking.

After 15 minutes of frustration, he gave up on that arm and went through the entire process on my other arm. Once again he met with resistance. By now I was starting to bruise and he was visibly upset and short-tempered. I was ready to check out and leave but that obviously wasn't an option. I was so relieved that Frankie wasn't there to see this.

I was taken back to my room and told they would have the hospital's PICC line specialist try again tomorrow. The next day a tall, handsome and kind fellow entered my room with a bandanna wrapped around his head; he looked more like a body builder than a doctor. He brought in a machine and said he would insert the line without requiring me to get out of bed. He was very confident he could get it right in and he did. From that point on, all my hospital admissions were based on his availability. Little did I know at the time that my veins were beginning to harden; specialists would frequently have a difficult time inserting the line due to all the scar tissue that had formed.

Once the line was in place, I assumed the rest of the hospital visit would be a breeze. I anticipated a few days to get my medicine IV level regulated and then I would be released to do my treatments at home for 7-10 days. I have allergies to some of the preservatives once used in the saline solutions that were used to flush out my PICC lines. In fact, I had such a severe allergic reaction one time in St. Louis that I went into anaphylactic shock. Thankfully Mom was with me during this visit and was able to call the nurse immediately who put me on Benadryl and oxygen. I don't know what I would have done without her because I didn't know what was happening. Each time I am admitted to the hospital now, I hang signs over my bed and on my door warning the nurses to be sure they use only preservative-free products.

One night a nurse came into the room to start my IV and I was on the phone not paying attention; I usually watch every move they make. Suddenly she injected the line and I felt a hot flush go through my body. My throat began to tighten and it felt like there was a vice gripping my neck. I looked at her and said, "That had preservatives?" She panicked and ran out of the room. Luckily there were orders written advising what to give me if this ever happened; once again I was injected with Benadryl and given oxygen. When Frankie called that night to ask how things were going, I told him I felt great!

~ ~ ~

The Tire Kicker

There is a saying I enjoy that accurately depicts life and business: 'If you want to make God laugh, tell Him your plans.' Nothing rang more true during those frustrating periods when Frankie and I tried to turn NatureSynergy into a successful, thriving business. We would spend hours and hours coming up with a plan of attack and within days would realize we had to change direction. There were so many times when we thought we were really on the precipice of something big that only resulted in disappointment.

One of the most frustrating things in business is that you can have the greatest ideas and products but if you can't afford to advertise them, you will quickly wither on the vine. We had so many great ideas but simply didn't have the funding to promote them. So we adopted the "one customer at a time" or "one massage therapist at a time" theory. While we were certain that the massage industry was our best chance for success, we still were lacking a plan. We realized we needed to learn more about this industry. Although Frankie had been a licensed massage therapist, all the rules and regulations had changed over the years.

We bought an industry trade publication and saw a large full-page ad by a massage therapy supply company that specialized in selling all the products that massage therapists and estheticians used. We noticed they carried thousands of body products but only a few odds and ends in skin care. It made sense because massage therapists don't really focus on their clients' faces. That work is left to the estheticians. However, massage therapists were licensed to touch faces and do light massage work on the heads, necks and faces of their clients. We thought it would be a great idea to market our line of skin care as a brand developed for massage therapists exclusively. This would give them a professional, concise line of products they could use and sell at retail prices which would enable them to profit even more.

We called the owner of the company in North Carolina who had run the ad in the magazine and asked to meet him. He agreed and seemed very interested in our concept. We were so excited about this potential opportunity that we put together color product brochures, a marketing plan which included our hands-on support for training and a phone number if his customers wanted to call us for further product information. If he bought into our line, we gave him our word that we would attend the upcoming industry's mega-trade show and work his booth for free.

We spent two days with this businessman who had hundreds and hundreds of massage therapists ordering from his catalog. We knew this was going to be a gold mine for us, especially when he invited us to the trade show which happened to be in Florida that particular year. We were "green" and accepted his invitation, even though he had not yet committed to our line of products.

Refusing to be deterred, we knew it was only a matter of time for our luck to change. We were willing to do just about anything to seal this deal. We literally did everything from helping build his booth, installing it before the show, loading and unloading trucks, standing for 12 hours three days in a row and even writing orders for his other product lines. We wanted to prove we were good partners. At the end of the show, we parted ways and agreed to talk the following week to get our 'deal' signed. One week passed. Then two and three weeks passed and before we knew it, months had passed. He had the same answer every week: "I'm still thinking about it but I do love you guys!" One of his inside customer service reps told us secretly that he was actually looking at another line of skin care which had a larger following; this rep didn't think he really had any interest in our line anymore but didn't have the nerve to tell us. As they say in business, he was a "tire-kicker" who was wasting our time and money.

Now we were obsessively driven to show this man what a mistake he'd made. During the period of trying to work together, he had a legal contract drawn up that was extremely lengthy; we didn't have the money to hire an attorney to review it. We figured we had little to lose and planned to sign it as written. Frankie recalled, however, one stipulation in the contract that stated we could not call on his competitor for three years if our business relationship ended. This man's competitor had a stronghold on the massage therapy market. Frankie looked at me and said, "Why aren't we calling on his competitor?"

However, we still didn't have an attractive, concise plan. We lacked marketing materials, nice packaging, case pricing, etc. Then the answer came to us when we needed it most. While we were at the large industry trade show, we noticed that all of the massage therapists in the country attended this show in order to take classes and receive continuing education credits every few years in order to keep their licenses current. What a powerful tool if we could combine our skin care with some type of a continuing education course. Further investigation showed that in order to be a provider of continuing education credits, you had to write and submit a course to the Massage Therapy

Accrediting Organization. There was a stringent review process involved and only a small number of the courses submitted every year were approved. Our chances were slim but all we needed was a chance.

We knew through previous research that massage therapists are licensed to do head and scalp massages. They can also do facial massages but many don't because they're unsure how to do them effectively. This is how we could make an impact in this industry! We could develop a facial massage technique and program which used our skin care products. Then the therapists could also retail the products for their customers to take home. It was something that hadn't been done before and it was an untapped market. They say in business that creating a demand is much harder than servicing a demand and that is so true. We had our work cut out for us.

While we were excited about this new plan, we felt extreme pressure to get this facet of our business going. We were still doing our green markets and small trade shows but we were only making enough to pay the bills. We located a few massage schools in the area and found an instructor who taught massage therapy. We met with her a few times to learn more about continuing education courses and in the process asked if she would work with us to develop a facial massage technique, one that we created which would work in tandem with our products. This couldn't be all fluff. We had to create a program that we could submit for continuing education credit approval that would be valid in the industry. It had to have a therapeutic outcome.

I don't think we slept for months as we worked on our new "Anti-Aging Facial Rejuvenation Through Facial Massage" technique and program. After we had the technique down, we then had to create support/training materials. We wrote manuals, created charts, devised educational materials, marketing materials and even filmed a professional video that demonstrated how to perform this technique on clients. We also developed a secondary program for therapists that was a 'Home Spa Party' program; this incorporated the new 'Anti-aging facial technique' and our skin care products as the take-home retail line. I did the writing and typing while Frankie did the printing and collating. Once this was accomplished, we went through the expensive, lengthy and tedious process of getting approval for continuing education credits.

~ ~ ~

The Expense of Success

Five months later our program was approved. Revenge can be a powerful motivator. Frankie picked up the phone and called Scrip, the large company in Illinois we would not have been allowed to work with had we signed a contract with the businessman in North Carolina. Frankie went right to the top. He asked to speak to the president, explained who we were, our program, our natural aloe vera based skin care line (which was a perfect fit for the wellness industry) and our desire to work with him. He also explained that we needed to have them partner with us and endorse our program so we could sell it to all of their massage therapy customers nationally.

The president was impressed and asked us to present our ideas to all of the decision-makers in the company. Frankie said "Yes!" immediately while I looked in the checkbook to see how we would pay for the flight!

We knew immediately upon meeting the president and his associates that this was going to be a perfect partnership. When we left three days later, we had a contract (only two pages in length) and an agreement that our line would be featured in their annual catalog. They were willing to aggressively market our program and help us reach our dreams. We were finally working with a very successful company that operated with integrity. We knew this would be the financial opportunity to change our lives. What we didn't think about was all the work ahead in servicing what quickly became over 200 consultants. We spent the next two years traveling to massage therapy schools, massage industry trade shows and private Home Spa parties in order to service our new family of customers.

   Along with success comes expense. When I was younger, I used to say to Dad, "Why don't you just buy this or go get that?" and he'd always say, "You don't understand. It takes money to make money." Over 30 years later, I now understand what he meant. Even though we were making a steady income, we were having trouble affording our growth. Our investor was placing larger orders for inventory, the consultants needed more marketing materials and our work load was growing and growing. Frankie took over the customer service and shipping needs, while I was in charge of marketing, sales and printing.

   It was too much work for the two of us but we couldn't afford to hire help. We were extremely fortunate that our product plant, Westport Labs, which was in St. Louis was a great partner. They understood our struggles and had seen the years of hard work we'd invested in trying to build our brand. They were a family-owned business that had faith in us. Either that or they pitied us! They agreed to extend us terms which were way beyond what any other product plant would do for their customers. To this day we recognize and appreciate that without them, we wouldn't have been able to stay in business.

   With our business growing at a nice rate, we found ourselves outgrowing our little apartment as it also became our office and warehouse. While we knew it would be a wise investment to buy a home of our own, we feared the thought of a mortgage if our business slowed down; this could mean not having enough money to grow. We were also worn out from literally working day and night for the last year without one day off. There was no time to slow down. Suddenly, our carefree, slow-paced life was crazy and hectic. It was apparent that Frankie's dream of walking the beach and writing poetry was slowly fading into the Florida sunset. What was even more apparent was the transformation in his work ethic. He had become a workaholic who wanted to get things done now! Did I do this to him or did he always harbor this entrepreneurial spirit that just needed a strong partner to push him forward?

We decided we needed a day off to relax and focus on one another. A friend who worked for me in our Beauty Source 1 salon strongly encouraged us to visit Naples, Florida that was just across the coast from Ft. Lauderdale. I had been there many years ago when I was married and remembered it as being a very elegant and upscale community with pristine beaches, high-end shops and esteemed restaurants.

Perhaps my friend thought we were doing better financially than we actually were but Frankie and I decided it would be good to get away for a day. This 'day trip' proved two things. Having big dreams on a small income can be a risky combination.

~ ~ ~

Get Busy Living or Get Busy Dying

I have probably seen the movie "Shawshank Redemption" ten times or more. One of my favorite lines is: 'You can get busy living or get busy dying.' I can relate to these words because when you live with a terminal disease, you have to make some decisions. Every day you wake up you have to ask yourself, "Are you going to let it consume you and take away your spirit or are you going to live life to the fullest and fight it with every ounce of energy you have?" Giving in and giving up has never been an option for me.

Many people (other than those who live with me day to day) think if I just slowed down I could be healthier and live longer. My hectic lifestyle raises eyebrows and I know it even has people talking behind my back at times. I know that any discussions about my health are done out of care and love. However, I firmly believe that I am still alive and living a good life because I don't slow down. I agree that my lifestyle decisions when I was younger were stupid; I regret that I didn't value taking care of myself and doing my treatments. I know that now. However, I thank God every day for watching over me and keeping me relatively healthy for so many years.

When someone asks how I am doing or feeling, I tell them I feel good and that I'm fine. When you have CF, you know that you are going to feel bad many days. You accept the fact that there will be tough days when it is hard to breathe. There will be more nights than not where you lie awake coughing for hours. There will be months when you will spend more time in the hospital on IV's than not. You expect to catch a cold which will likely turn into pneumonia. That is something you live with day in and day out. However, I think all of us CFers have a gauge we use that reminds us how we are really doing. It is our pulmonary function test which is done every few months. This measures the amount of air you can breathe in, the amount you can blow out in the first few seconds and ultimately how much air you can breathe out altogether. It gives you an idea of how quickly you are losing lung volume.

Back in the 70's, my FEV1 (forced expiratory volume in 1 second) was in the 90th percentile. By the 90's it was in the high 80th percentile which was something that amazed the doctors. I was fortunate that it didn't decline much. By 2007 it was in the high 70's and now in the year 2012, I am at 59% and slowly declining. Things changed for me dramatically in 2009 when I started seeing a sharper decline in my numbers. I have been told by my doctors that it is not until my FEV1 drops to 30 % that I would be considered a candidate for a lung transplant. According to all my doctors, my numbers are still quite amazing for my age. This isn't to say that I'm not sad or concerned about the decline in my lung volume. I am and it's something I'm conscious of every single day. I don't want to get worse and in my mind I still think I can and will beat this disease.

I take my health care very seriously now. My doctors and nurses laugh when I come in because I'm obsessed with doing anything I can do to be as healthy as possible. It is actually a joke in the office because I have a superstitious routine. I have to spend the night before my appointment in a hotel within a few miles of the hospital. I have to eat protein before I go but not to the point where I am too full to breathe, I make Frankie wait outside the room for the first few blows, I won't talk business on the way to the doctors' offices because it might make me uptight or stressed . . . and the list goes on and on.

Then once I complete my test and get the results, I begin my interrogation process with my team of doctors, my nurse, Lisa, my respiratory therapist, Bob, my nutritionist, Jody, and the rest of the devoted and caring group who have now taken care of me for many years. I would be lost without them. Besides being so closely involved with my care, they are responsible for keeping all of us CFers motivated and hopeful about our future. I have to ask the same questions I asked only two months prior and then tell them all my new theories about my disease and how to treat it. Lisa just rolls her eyes as I repeat, "But what if we did this?" or "What if we tried that?" or "Did you look at the option of?" Frankie just shakes his head and says, "Welcome to my world." But when I ask my doctors what else I can do, they have all had the same answer over the last 40 + years: "Keep doing whatever you're doing because it is obviously working." So that is why I always come back to the same conclusion in terms of how to prolong my life: to get busy living which is exactly what I do.

~ ~ ~

Paradise

Frankie had never been to Naples so I was really looking forward to our little get away. I'm filled with a great sense of happiness watching him experience things for the first time. Our childhoods were dramatically different. His mother was a single parent raising three boys on her own while my sisters and I were blessed with a privileged life that included road trips, elegant meals and shopping adventures. I wouldn't say our family was wealthy while growing up but Mom and Dad made sure we had whatever we needed or wanted in life. We weren't spoiled but we were well taken care of in every possible way. So even to this day when Frankie is enjoying doing something excessive (like buying the best seats at a Red Sox game) I complain a little (that's my job, isn't it?) although I'm secretly beaming inside watching him enjoy his life.

My girlfriend insisted that we check out an area in Naples called Fiddler's Creek. She described it as being a luxurious gated community with magnificent swimming pools, golf courses, a tennis club and two on-site restaurants nestled in a protected wildlife preserve. We were anxious to take a tour and stopped at the sales center first upon arriving. We were given the impression that all the units for sale were only brand new ones and that there were no resale units available. When we were given the sales sheets with the layouts of all the units, we were absolutely in awe of this beautiful gated community. It was unlike anything we'd ever seen; unfortunately the prices were depressingly way beyond what we could afford at this point in our careers. If that wasn't discouraging enough, we weren't in a position to build a new condo or home and this was the only option presented.

We didn't ever discuss it but I know we both felt the same way as we drove away from what we both thought was a piece of paradise. We felt a little dejected but thought it would be fun to spend the rest of the day on Marco Island at the beach; it was so charming and we felt like we were on a small self-contained island with all the amenities of city life. It was filled with boutiques, restaurants, theaters, beaches and a sidewalk that ran the entire length of the island where you could skate, bike or walk for miles. I pictured us living in this secluded and peaceful area that was so serene, you could hear nature speaking.

We stopped to eat lunch at a little sandwich shop on the island and Frankie picked up a newspaper. An ad for Fiddler's Creek was plastered on the center page with the heading in bold type: 'Resale homes available now' with prices that were much less than what we'd been shown. We called the agent listed on the ad and luckily he answered. We told him we were in town for two hours and asked if he could show us the few units he was advertising.

Within thirty minutes we met our agent, Mike. He showed us two units that were nice but not what we'd envisioned one day owning. When we walked through the third unit, it immediately felt like our dream home. It was a perfect size with vaulted ceilings, an open floor plan with a large great room and a beautiful lanai which overlooked palm trees and lush vegetation. I know it seems like we are both somewhat impulsive but really I'm not. I'm an analyzer and I agonize over even the smallest decisions. I spend hours at the grocery store in the olive oil and cereal aisles virtually paralyzed by all the choices and afraid to make a commitment. Inexplicably, I can buy a home in fifteen minutes! When I see it and know it, I want it.

The next thing I knew, we were signing papers and making an offer. We felt an instant connection with Mike and his wife, Maureen, who helped us through the process. We quickly had calculated our payments and if we could come up with the down payment then we would be fine as long as our business was successful. As it was, we were doing well and were at least making a steady income. We had hundreds of consultants and Scrip was a great partner helping us secure more business with their reps. We were used to getting orders daily through emails but most of the larger orders placed by Scrip were over the phone. They would give us the information of all the new sign-ups and then we would prepare the orders and drop ship individually. We would typically get a few orders a day and some days as many as three or four which was thrilling.

The day we were driving back from Fiddler's Creek our email 'in box' was dinging every few minutes. We figured it was spam because it was one order after the next. We both wanted to believe our hard work was finally paying off but we knew from past experiences that we shouldn't get too excited. By the time we got home we had over 22 orders and they all looked legitimate. We were flabbergasted and although we were ecstatic, we knew there had to be a reason we were getting so many orders suddenly. The suspense was too much.

So we opened one of the email order confirmations and reviewed the customer's contact information. We randomly looked at one from California and decided to call her and thank her for the order. Then we could find out how she heard about our line and try to make sense of our sudden onslaught of orders.

She told us that she was an HSN customer and a member of the HSN community message board. We acted like we knew what she was talking about but Frankie and I weren't live TV shopping channel watchers or buyers. She said there was a post on the message board written by a lady who had raved about our skin care line (which was not called Ice Elements Skin Care at that time). The woman explained there is a big community of skin care devotees on that board and if one person really recommends something then all women have to try it. We were shocked.

The first call we made was to Mom and Dad. We were so proud to announce that we finally had made it. We were so eager to show them we were going to be okay. After years of doing trade shows, green markets and consultant home spa parties, all it took was one post written on a message board in order to put our business in high gear. At the time, we thought this was the start of the end of our hard work. We thought the orders would now come pouring in for the rest of our lives. Wrong! Our work was just beginning.

The next day we got good news from Mike, our agent at Fiddler's Creek. The seller had accepted our offer. I immediately started scribbling notes and calculating expenses. I added up the cost of moving and buying the condo. I'm not sure I ever really came up with a budget because I knew we would just have to work hard enough to make it work. We had a lot of packing to do and would need to hire a moving company. We gave ourselves a few weeks to get organized and packed and before we knew it, it was moving day.

That morning Frankie got a call from his brother. His mother had a heart attack and he needed to fly to Rhode Island immediately to see her. At the time, he had a somewhat strained relationship with her and they hadn't seen one another in years. I had talked to her on the phone but had never met her. It was too late to cancel the movers so I stayed behind and led the procession to Fiddler's Creek in Naples. I had such mixed emotions about his leaving because this was going to be the first home Frankie had ever owned. I wanted him to be there to enjoy the whole experience. However, it gave me time to get everything put away and set up to surprise him. He came home five days later and I finally slept five days later. We had our own little piece of paradise now.

~ ~ ~

Ponds

There is nothing like watching pure joy in the eyes of someone you love. Even though Frankie had seen our new home in Naples, it had been a short visit. When he returned home, he was stunned to see the transformation in what was now our home together. All the work required to get it ready in time for his arrival was well worth it. We actually had an office now. We still only had one very old computer but we had room for two and that would be our first priority. What had not changed was the copious amount of materials we used for our home spa parties and continuing education program. Boxes and boxes of inventory lined the entire perimeter of our dining room and living room areas. We now had more room for "stuff."

We promised one another that we would start taking time to enjoy all the amenities in our gorgeous community and if nothing else, we wouldn't work weekends. As we both took a pinkie swear to this promise, deep down I was thinking, "How can we take time to relax when we still don't have any expendable income?"

Frankie, who was very different from the Frankie I met a few years earlier was secretly thinking the same thing. Even though we were experiencing nice growth and adding more and more consultants to our program every day, we still needed to reach a critical mass in order to have long-term security. While we were still getting some residual orders from the rush of HSN message board customers, they were down to a trickle. We found ourselves daydreaming aloud and wondering what it would be like to have plentiful orders coming in every day. The reality was that we didn't have any type of budget to advertise. We wondered if perhaps an investor was the way to go; we needed someone who could infuse money into our company and help us become more visible.

One day I was telling Mom that we were considering looking for an investor. She reminded me that she had a friend whose son lived in Boca. He was a "marketing whiz" who invested in start-up companies. If nothing else, perhaps he could give us some ideas. At this point, we had so few options that we called him and arranged to meet in a week.

Frankie and I put together an impressive power point presentation along with gift bags of our products and a comprehensive business plan. We were certain he'd be impressed. When we arrived at his home, we were greeted by a nanny who escorted us to a magnificent study. I had never met this man before so I didn't know what to expect. As the oversized office chair turned slowly around, there was a guy sitting in it with his feet barely touching the ground and a huge cigar protruding from his lips. Wait a minute! I could read the look on Frankie's face which mimicked my thoughts exactly: "How did a guy so young make it so big? It's not fair." But we knew that nothing in life or business was always fair. What was encouraging though was that he was this successful.

We offered to take him and his wife to lunch and discuss business during our meal; he suggested a place he enjoyed. When we arrived, I noticed that the least expensive meal was $32 and that was for the Kobe Beef Burger. I kicked Frankie under the table and rolled my eyes in the direction of the menu. He knew I was worried about the price but he gave me a "Don't worry about it" look.

After two hours of our talking and receiving somewhat of a blank stare, the gentleman finally spoke. I didn't hear a lot of what he said after, "You need help. The packaging is not attractive and the formulas are not unique." His wife chimed in that women would never warm up to the idea of a gel exfoliator like our 2 Minute Miracle. He told us to look at the Ponds brand because they knew how to do it right. Ponds? We drove all this way and spent $137 for lunch to hear that? I couldn't wait to tell Mom she really missed the target on this one.

We were cordial and thanked him for his time and expert opinions. He was kind and said he wished he had better news for us but we needed to rethink our brand and strategy if we were to be successful. Those closing words were all we needed to hear; this fueled us to work even harder if that was at all possible.

~ ~ ~

Then and Now

Frankie, you are not the same man Shelly saw at the stoplight. At that point in your life, you weren't worried about job security or plans for the future. Now she can't get you to slow down and take a break. When did you change? Why did you change? Even more, who are you today compared to the man you were before Shelly came into your life?

Beth

Transformation

Truthfully, Beth, I am pretty much the same exact man Shelly saw at the stoplight. I was simply given a gift the day we met. It was a good time in my life when we started dating. I was finally somewhat normal in that I wasn't chasing women and going out all night.

I truly believe God said to me, "Shelly is your special gift. Your future is now taken care of and secure." Until then I never worried about it, getting older and having enough money to survive in later years. The truth . . . I am still that way. At 48 years old I still live in the moment. Dating Shelly since 2001 and then being married since 2010 has actually confirmed this for me. Her challenges with CF is a daily reminder that life is short. I really do believe in smelling the roses and always living life to the fullest … today!

If I only had $100 in my pocket at this moment, I would rather buy Shelly a $60 shirt that she loves, get her a $20 manicure and spend the last $20 for two drinks as we watch a beautiful sunset. I love to see her happy. Savings? I simply would not be disciplined enough to save or plan for the future. If it wasn't for Shelly, we would only have a few bucks in the bank BUT Shelly would have a diamond necklace, the best clothes money can buy, a personal trainer, a personal massage therapist, a chef to cook her meals, a personal assistant AND we would travel to exotic places and visit children's hospitals which is something she really wants to do. Problem … we need money to do all this.

I work my tail off and stay focused because of her. She is a finely tuned machine and let's nothing stand in her way. Her work ethic and vision is unstoppable, incredible, outstanding and ridiculous! I work hard to keep up with her. We are a fantastic team. We work so well together and enjoy each other so much it's easy. She is a locomotive train with a vision that says "Get the heck out of my way as I come down this track."

She has a deadly disease yet NEVER uses this as an excuse in her personal life or professional life where she has succeeded in every business venture. She gets up each morning, coughs up blood, does two uncomfortable treatments (and two more treatments later in the day), barely breathes with her daily congestion, goes to the gym for two hours and runs 3-5 miles, worries each day if the cold she may be getting could kill her, coughs up more blood after the gym, comes home and then works for the next 12 hours on her skin care company, her radio show, our second infomercial we are creating, helping friends daily who call her for advice, making me dinner regularly and washing our clothes. On top of that she has spent the last six months writing a book.

Why did I change? I changed because of Shelly. I have to keep up with her! After reading about all that she does in a day, how would I feel if I took the day off? If I didn't work hard each day, I would feel like the biggest loser. I work hard because she has instilled this quality in me.

Because of Shelly, I am a man who is much more compassionate, kind, appreciative of the small things in life and grateful for every precious day. I smile more and thank God each and every day for what I have. I feel like I finally have a purpose and much more control of my destiny. With business/work, I always thought it was the other guy who would hire me and give me a job. Now we are truly successful and even though we have no employees, we are in control.

~ ~ ~

Someone Wins the Car

When Frankie and I were doing our trade shows, we met a gal, Carol, who also had her own make-up business. The company was small like ours and she, too, had aspirations of growing into a large national company one day. When we were talking about our strategies, I mentioned that I would love to get our products on HSN. We all laughed because that was obviously the goal for thousands, if not millions of other companies. Then Carol said, "Hey, someone wins the car!"

We loved that saying and it was true. No one expects to hit it big on a game show but in the end, someone wins the car. Why not us?

The next day I told Frankie we should look at the HSN message board to see the post where the women were talking about our products. We were barely familiar with HSN and the entire live television shopping channels and certainly had never been to their message board. Through a search, we found a message board with multiple categories that included everything from houseware items to skin care products. We were shocked that the post about our products was on the very first page of the beauty section. What was even more exciting was that apparently the woman whom we had called a few weeks earlier (the one who told us about this post) had now posted that she spoke to us, said what great people we were and how Frankie helped her with her product selection. There were other women with nicknames (so you can remain anonymous) who were also posting back with positive responses and praise.

This was too exciting and we had to parlay this into something beyond the message board post. I looked at Frankie and said, "Let's call the main number at HSN, talk to the beauty department and tell them about our products." He tilted his head sideways and raised his eyebrows the way he does whenever I say something preposterous, and said, "Shelly, you don't just call HSN. They have procedures. Otherwise everyone would be calling them all the time."

I knew he was right but in truth I never really heard the rest of his sentence. My mind was made up that I was going to get us in there somehow. I looked on-line and realized Frankie was right. They had an entire page on their site which laid out specific details in submitting your product for review. The process sounded like it could take forever to get an answer and worse yet that answer could be a "no." That just didn't work for me.

I went on-line and found mounds of articles on HSN. One article included a quote from one of the buyers, Christine, who worked in the beauty division. I called the headquarters and punched 0 for the operator and asked to be connected to Christine. The gal on the other end of the phone identified herself and said she was the assistant to Christine who was in a meeting with all the buyers. At that moment, I decided I had to somehow convince her to help me. If I merely left a message, I knew there was a good chance it would go unanswered.

I asked the assistant if she was in front of a computer at that moment. She was. I asked her to go to the HSN message board and click on the skin care section. I then explained I had a skin care line and although I was not selling on HSN, my line was selling well in spas and to estheticians and massage therapists. I emphasized that over the last three weeks I had been inundated with hundreds of orders from HSN customers. (Okay, so I embellished slightly.) I explained that these customers were talking about us on their message HSN boards. (This part was true). I said I hated to see HSN customers buying a line of products that was not even featured on HSN and stressed they (HSN) were missing out on sales. Of course, I didn't stop to think how silly this must have sounded. HSN processes thousands and thousands of orders daily; their missing out on my few sales probably didn't affect their ability to thrive! Yet I had to make it sound monumental in the scheme of things. I assured the young woman that I was not a nut bag but a very passionate and motivated skin care developer. She started reading aloud the posts; she was impressed and said she would tell the buyer when she got out of her meeting. By now I was actually begging for her help.

I asked her to please print all the message board posts, take them into the meeting and tell those in attendance that there was a lady on the phone who owned a skin care line and wanted their help in boosting sales. This was another ridiculous statement that came out of my mouth! I said I would call her back in a bit to see how things went. She said she couldn't promise anything but I told her that she was doing me a favor I would never forget.

I waited for what seemed like a week but it was really about two hours. I called her back and said, "Hi, it's me again. I'm so sorry to bother you but were you able to take copies of the posts into the meeting?" Once again I assured her that I was not a stalker or crazed woman. She said that she had and explained our conversation to the buyers; she said Christine would call me. I thanked her repeatedly and then interrogated her a little longer to ask what the odds were that Christine would call. She said it was possible and to be patient.

I've always been a person who wants to know my odds. It's still a joke in my family because when I was young and the evening news reporter announced "potential" school closings for the next day, I had to know my odds that school would be cancelled. I couldn't merely take the weather guy's opinion. I needed to go right to the top. For some reason, I had my principal's home phone number (don't recall how I got that). I had my brother-in-law, Davey, call pretending he was the father of a school child who needed to know what chance there was of a cancellation.

We even came up with the fictitious name of 'Buz wa Zee' for my brother-in-law's company. I'm sure we didn't fool my principal each time but I did get a better inkling for the odds of not having school.

A few weeks later I still had not heard from Christine so I called her. She took my call and I went through my story with her one more time. As we were talking, Frankie was pacing in the background. He was motioning, holding up pieces of paper with key words he wanted me to mention and towards the end was down on one knee with his hands in the begging position. When Christine told me to send our products to her along with detailed information, I gave Frankie the thumbs-up sign. You would have thought I said we were starting on Monday; he yelled out a "YES!" so loud that I had to explain it to Christine. She got a good laugh out of it and we were on our way!

~ ~ ~

Taking a Chance

When my conversation with Christine ended, she said she needed three weeks to evaluate our information and for me to call her back on a specific date. Frankie and I counted down every minute of every day until it was time. I dialed her number and on the third ring her recorder picked up. The message said she would be out of the office for three months on maternity leave! It went on to direct any callers to one of the other beauty buyers. Our hearts sank. After all this, we were back to square one.

Luckily Christine had mentioned in passing another beauty buyer's name. We had nothing to lose so we called him, explained our situation and history and that we had hoped to meet with Christine. Greg, the buyer, was very kind and sounded intrigued by our brand and story. He said he'd gather all the information we sent Christine, would review it and call us back in a few weeks. Even though this was another wait, he did call back as promised and asked us to come to St. Petersburg and meet with him and some of his team so we could do our "dog and pony show." We were scheduled to go there in two weeks. All we needed was a chance to be seen. We knew in our minds that if we got in there, we would not leave without a "yes."

Our big day arrived and we met with all the folks at HSN who were in the beauty department. The two-hour meeting was very positive. They liked everything except our packaging which they thought needed updating. We agreed. They said they'd look at the schedule for the remainder of the year and see if there was any opening for a few shows as a trial run. Even if there was an opening, it would be practically impossible for us to get ready but we acted like it would all be a breeze. I was even more overwhelmed by the reality that we didn't have excess cash for new packaging, inventory stock, marketing materials and a website that were all required to be successful.

In the event this did work out we decided to meet with the owners at Westport Labs, with our screen printer, Poge, and most importantly our accountant, Verletta. We had a close relationship with everyone and thought of them like partners. We told them about the potential opportunity and the challenges we would face financially if this were to come to fruition. Due to our lack of cash flow, we would not be able to pay our suppliers for 60-90 days. They were all eager to help.

A few weeks later Greg called with what he thought was bad news. In looking at the HSN schedule, there were no opportunities for us to be on for at least another year. He did, however, mention that they had a secondary station, America's Store, which many current HSN vendors appear on after they do their HSN shows. He explained this station had a much smaller viewing audience and was seldom used as a launching pad for new brands because the volume was so low which meant a great deal of risk for a vendor who could potentially ship in thousands of products and perhaps only sell a small number. Frankie had the buyer on speaker phone at the time and in tandem both Frankie and I said, "We don't care. We'll take it!" In our eyes, taking a risk was the opportunity to grow our business.

When I look back at our first launch on America's Store, I'm embarrassed how little I knew about live TV. I thought there would be some type of stringent training course but I suppose since this station was traditionally not a launch pad for new brands, those who appeared were usually seasoned vendors. Not me. I was hooked up to a microphone and had an earpiece stuck in my ear. The only training I was given was, "Look at the lights on top of each camera." This indicated where I should focus since there were three or four different cameras involved.

Fortunately it didn't matter. Apparently we did great. We sold nearly 60 total units and for us this was big. We were used to selling 20 units in a day at our green markets so to sell this many units in one hour was a real milestone. We continued to do shows on America's Store for the next seven months which helped grow our customer base and enabled me to hone my live TV skills.

As we became more immersed in our HSN business, we had less time to spend growing our Home Spa Party consultant business. We also didn't have the time to work with Scrip who was still promoting our accreditation program for massage therapists. We finally decided it was in our best interest to look at selling this entire division. There was a massage therapist we'd worked closely with over the last few years and she also had very close ties with Scrip. When she expressed interest in buying it, we all wanted to make this transition as quick and easy as possible. We sat down together and drafted our own agreement. Now Frankie and I could focus all of our time and energy on Ice Elements Skin Care.

~ ~ ~

No Joke

One day in January of 2005, we got a call from someone on our buying team. There were a few spots open on April 1st on the HSN station and they wanted to give us a shot at launching Ice Elements. Frankie took the call as I watched him pace the floor and repeatedly say, "You are kidding, right? Is this going to be an April Fool's joke?" When he got off the phone and told me what they said, I kept repeating, "You are kidding me! Is this a bad joke?" We dreamed of this day but really never knew if the seven months of spending well over $25,000 (for the cost of products, models, hair and makeup, clothing, etc.) to make $20,000 would ever pay off. It did!

Now there was real work to do. When we got our show purchase order, we couldn't believe it. The size of the order was huge and so much had to be done to get it ready. My greatest concern was my hair! What color should it be? What should I wear? Should I whiten my teeth? What if I coughed? What if I was sick that day? I wanted everything to be perfect.

For the next two months I wrote notes to myself incessantly. I had 50 pages of things I wanted to remember to say on air. In actuality, had I mentioned everything I would have needed three hours per show. I kept rehearsing my notes and talking to myself in the mirror, in the shower, on the treadmill every morning and even in my sleep. I would get out of bed in the middle of the night to jot down a few more things I couldn't forget to say. I also started watching HSN 24/7. I wanted to understand how other vendors presented their products; I wanted to see if there were any "tricks" I could pick up. During this process I also became a very loyal HSN shopper. Knowing as an "insider" how serious they are about quality and value, it gave me an appreciation for shopping with them.

A few days prior to our launch date, there were many pre-show meetings that included legal meetings (you have to be able to substantiate any claim you make on air), production meetings, host training meetings, model meetings, planning meetings and so on. I bought all my models pretty blue shirts with our Ice Elements logo and Frankie designed and ordered a large custom-made Ice Cube with our logo in the middle where we could display our products. We also thought it would be a nice touch to have a live aloe plant on the set as well since this was the basis of our line, along with the natural protein that grows in the glacier region.

~ ~ ~

Record Breaker

It was now show time. I had my makeup and hair done in the Green Room, my models were ready and Frankie was helping set up everything. Once my microphone was in place, I walked down to the live set. We had an 11 p.m. show which is considered prime air time. I heard the producer count down in my ear and the next thing I knew we were live and I was selling and doing my thing.

Everything was going as planned. What I didn't expect was the responses from viewers. During my demonstration, I was watching the live monitor that indicated how many calls and orders we were getting. I looked over and saw what I thought to be thousands of numbers "in the red." Even though there can be 40, 60 or even hundreds of live operators at any one time answering calls and processing orders as fast as they can, there are times when the call volume is greater than the number of orders they can process. So the customer is on hold. This is what being "in the red" means. I think I was so shocked that I forgot what I was doing temporarily and just stared at the numbers. I questioned if I was seeing things correctly. Could we actually be getting a thousand orders and more? The sheer excitement was electrifying and kicked my energy level to an all-time high.

At the end of our show, we got an email from our assistant buyer who said we had broken a record for the highest sales of a new skin care launch! We had other shows scheduled for 5 o'clock the next morning which meant I had to be up by 2 a.m. and over to the studio by 3 a.m. I don't think Frankie and I slept a minute. We were deliriously happy. We thought this was the way it would always be. This was easy!

~ ~ ~

The Thrill of Victory and the Agony of Defeat

If you are on HSN, how could there be any "agony of defeat?" Frankie and I quickly learned that there are no guarantees you will have a good show or visit. It's reality. You wait three months to be back on air so you pour your heart and soul into every visit. The pressure and experience of live TV is not for the faint of heart.

The HSN hosts are nothing short of brilliant. Their lines are not scripted. They are seasoned and sharp professionals who make it look easy as they go from selling skin care, to jewelry, to copier scanners to bison meat. Their job is to drive the sale and allow the guest to give the product presentation. Before any of my visits, I send samples and a letter to the hosts I'll have, in the hopes they'll use the product in advance. I spend a great deal of time preparing my show notes; a virtual play-by-play of the way I want things to flow. Our primary models, Kara, Ingerborg, Carolyn and Bev are essential to successful shows. They are my security blanket; we have all worked together a long time and have become friends.

Although Frankie isn't in front of the camera, he takes care of the many things that need to be done behind the scene. He is also the "numbers guy" and not one detail gets past him. He attends all the pre-show meetings and works closely with the producers and the stage people. As the show segment begins, he watches from the Green Room where he takes notes, analyzes call volume and yells as if I can hear him giving me directions. His attention to detail is invaluable because it enables us to tweak the next show accordingly. We have a deal that after every show he has to walk out and say "Good job" and look sincerely pleased. Then only after a few hours is he able to tell the truth. Maintaining a high level of confidence on my part is so critical that any negative comments can bring me down quickly.

At the end of each segment, I feel emotionally drained whether things went well or not. When I get a longer break between shows I usually do my breathing treatments and wear my percussion vest. After Frankie percusses my back and sides, I do my three-mile run. Then I shower again and head back to the studio for the next show. While many would question working at such a high stress level, we are thankful every day to have this opportunity.

~ ~ ~

The Low High Horse

Everyone who lives with CF knows to expect the unexpected. I'm normally able to disguise moments when I'm running a fever or having more difficulty breathing, but one day in particular stands out vividly in my mind; so much, in fact, that it saddens me to even think about it because my words hurt Frankie.

Prior to this particular visit on HSN, I had just finished 21 days of being on a PICC line in the hospital and at home. I still felt sick and was running a fever. My throat was raw and I was so hoarse that it took every ounce of effort I had to push out a sound. I had numerous nebulizer treatments to do before going on air and was coughing up blood. I felt so down but didn't want to say anything. I didn't want to give in to feeling so ill because a successful show is 70% mental. You need to truly believe you will soar during your shows; otherwise, the pace and stress of live TV can tear you apart.

Frankie and I got into a little disagreement about something that was business- related. We have the ability to disagree then hug and put it behind us. This time he was so frustrated with me that he said, "Oh, Shelly, get off your high horse on that!"

I lost it. I started sobbing and threw my hairbrush across the room. In a voice that was barely audible, I screamed, "Oh yeah, lucky me, sitting on a real high horse. I can't breathe, can't speak, am coughing up blood and have to be on the air in two hours!"

Frankie ran over to hold me and kept repeating, "I am so sorry, I know- I am so sorry." We clung to each other and cried together. It makes me cry thinking about it. We both were so frustrated with my health; my disease had knocked me down physically and both of us emotionally. I had no choice but to do what I've always done. I got up again. As Frankie and I high-fived, I said, "Let's go have a great show" and we did.

~ ~ ~

The Clampetts Hit the Road

With our first shows under our belts and a successful launch, we were now on our way to becoming an approved HSN vendor/ partner. We had follow-up meetings with our buying team and immediately began planning our next rotation of shows which would be in another two months. There was so much to do, so much to coordinate and I was still so new to the process. It wasn't until a few years later that I learned to calm down and enjoy the journey; I eventually realized there would always be things out of my control.

Frankie and I became machines pumping out hours and hours of work every day; I was often so exhausted that I would literally fall asleep at my keyboard. Once you do well on live TV on a station as visible as HSN, it opens the door for many opportunities. There are live TV shopping channels in other countries that function very similarly to HSN and many HSN vendors present in other countries. While not as large or successful in many cases, they are still a lucrative source of revenue if you want to take the chance and make the effort.

We had heard about a live shopping channel in Canada and thought that might be a good place to start because we wouldn't need dual language labels. We already had plenty of product inventory in stock and thought we could implement what we'd done on HSN the previous two years. We asked one of our close HSN friends for the name of a buyer at The Shopping Channel in Canada and she was eager to help.

After months of negotiations, product review, completion of all the international forms and customs paperwork, we were approved to appear on their show in March of 2007. Frankie thought it would be fun to do a road trip. Plus it would give us a chance to drive to Michigan to see his brother and family and then drive to Canada.

The atmosphere at the Canadian station was very different. All show segments were one hour and there was a laid-back atmosphere; it was refreshing not to feel any pressure. After two days of shows, we sold out of nearly all the items we'd shipped ahead of time. Although it was a great success, we agreed that it would be detrimental to my health to continue working at HSN and the Canadian station. Our business was growing with HSN and it was becoming increasingly challenging to keep up with the demand for our products. Adding another venue at that point could potentially have hindered our growth with them.

Driving thousands of miles with someone is a wonderful way to know if you are really compatible. Our first long road trip to Canada proved that we are. Some of our fondest memories have been spent driving throughout the country in a car loaded with clothes, my vest and breathing machine, food, a laptop and lots of gum for Frankie. There is something thrilling about being carefree and figuring out a plan as you go.

Our close friends and relatives always ask the same thing: "Don't you two ever get sick of spending time together?" We both answer the same way: "No, not really." The truth is I am almost embarrassed by how much time we do spend together and how much we love every moment of it. Don't get me wrong. There are times when we totally annoy each other. Frankie chomps his gum too loudly while he's driving and I never stop analyzing and planning what we should do next. We know it and laugh about it.

We try to do a road trip every year since we can basically run our business from anywhere when we aren't doing live shows on HSN. Just like the Clampetts on 'The Beverly Hillbillies' we love loading up the car with what looks like everything we own and hitting the road.

~ ~ ~

A Magical Moment

Although we were on the road to success with HSN and barely had a minute to breathe, we felt like we weren't taking full advantage of our potential for growth. Frankie told me repeatedly that we'd never have to worry about our future if we could somehow market our 2 Minute Miracle Gel to masses of people. He was actually frustrated because we didn't have the money to advertise in a big way with an infomercial and repeatedly said, "We have the ultimate infomercial product."

The thought about "our future" means something different to me than it does to him, especially the older I get and experience more valleys than peaks with my health. My goal for the future is to have security for both of us as we age. Quite possibly he will outlive me (barring any unusual turn of events) and I want the peace of mind that he will be well taken care of his entire life. So working hard now to have a bright and financially stable future is of the utmost importance to me. When I tell him this, he tells me I'm so stubborn that I will outlive everyone we know.

One day I received an email that was sent in mass to a number of skin care and beauty companies. The email was in regards to a report that could be purchased which included new data about the buying habits of 'today's women.' It was very in-depth information published by a large reputable company, 'The Beauty Company.' I thought about all the people who were on this email list that had been sent by Alisa, the president of the company. I realized she would undoubtedly have contacts throughout the beauty industry and would be a good contact for us.

I sent her an email introducing ourselves and our company along with a link to one of our of our 2 Minute Miracle Gel show segments on HSN shows which was posted on YouTube. I knew this would grab her attention because everyone who sees the live demo is intrigued. I concluded by telling her we wanted to expand our business and said we would be forever grateful if she would share any ideas or insight.

Alisa called two days later. She was so interested in our product and story that she asked if we would be attending the annual Las Vegas Beauty Trade Show. She said everyone in the industry attended this and we could meet her as well as many other contacts. I shared our desire to reach the masses through an infomercial but explained we didn't have the money to invest in the production and air time. She mentioned that the world's largest infomercial company, Guthy-Renker (GRC) would be attending as well as other private investors. Guthy Renker! We couldn't believe it. Everyone knew Guthy-Renker from all the infomercials that feature big-name celebrities. The chance to meet anyone from that company seemed too good to be true. We were going to Vegas.

A few days prior to leaving, she called to say that she had set up an appointment for us with Jennifer, one of the representatives from Guthy-Renker. We were told we would only have about 30 minutes of her time because she had many appointments with other companies as well. We understood and were grateful for the opportunity.

We arrived in Vegas late and I was really fatigued. Flying is always a challenge for me but especially with a three-hour time change that really interfered with my medicine schedule. The next morning we headed to the convention center and met Jennifer. Frankie and I were so excited that I don't know how she followed anything we said. As soon as one of us started a sentence the other would interrupt and add more explanation. She just smiled and followed along like she was watching a fast ping-pong match.

We demonstrated our star product, the 2 Minute Miracle on the back of her hand and she was visibly overwhelmed by the results. Nearly three hours later, she said her trip was a success by finding us. She added that she would present our product to her team in California. She also said we would definitely hear from her within three weeks. This proved to be three very long weeks for us.

Now the best thing we could do was relax, take in the sites of Las Vegas and enjoy the rest of our evening. So we did. We ate at 'Olives' which is located in the Bellagio and sits elevated over the famous dancing fountains. I had told Frankie about this place for years and said my dream was to go there together. It was so romantic and when the choreographed fountains danced to the song "Time to Say Goodbye" by Andrea Bocelli and Sarah Brightman, I cried. The music, the words, the grandeur and power of the fountains left me breathless. Frankie looked over at me and tilted his head the way he always does in his sweet caring way as his eyes welled with tears. This was a magical moment and a memory we would hold dear in our hearts forever.

~ ~ ~

False Alarm

Two weeks passed and we got a call from Jennifer. Guthy-Renker was very interested in us and our product. The company asked us to fly out to meet them and talk about a possible deal. We had the things they looked for in a brand. This was a dream come true; it was even harder for my dad to grasp. He had more "what if" questions than I did because of his natural questioning nature and concern for my well-being. As excited as I was about this news, I was scared. Not about the business side of this new venture but the toll it could potentially take on me physically. When I was younger, I never thought about this and went for the gusto. That was no longer the case. I had to think about my health and the possible repercussions.

Flying to LA would be exciting but it would be another plane trip. This meant more exposure to germs and the change in cabin pressure that was hard on my lungs. I also worried about the difference in time zones and getting adjusted to my treatment schedule changing. I knew this concern weighed on Frankie because he mentioned it a few times as we celebrated the good news. Sometimes it is the small things in life that can validate your love for one another and this was another instance when Frankie proved his total love for me. He told me repeatedly that even though this was our big break, he would give it all up if it was too much for me. Of course, I said, "It wasn't too much." Deep down, however, I was worried.

In June of 2007 we flew to LA to meet the entire GRC team and then after four months of intense negotiations, stressful contract revisions and hundreds of conference calls, we signed a deal. The contract gave them three years to shoot and market our show. When you live with CF, three years sounds like a lifetime. Although I plan to live a long time, I never plan that far ahead.

Since we were already an existing brand on TV, GRC trusted our ideas and instincts and relied on us heavily throughout the development stage of the project. It was a full year of ground work that had to be established in order for all of us to get to the point of writing a script and shooting our infomercial. Although Frankie and I were not famous, they began treating us like stars from day one. When we traveled we flew first class. They arranged for our lodging at the beautiful Lowes hotel on the beach in Santa Monica and made sure we had transportation, fine meals and entertainment during our downtime. At night, Frankie and I would sit on the deck overlooking the Santa Monica Pier and pinch ourselves to make sure it was real. Although we were having a great time, the pace was wearing me down more than I wanted to admit.

We had become close friends with one of our producers, Coleen, and her boss, Elliott. Coleen was always looking out for me because she had a girlfriend whose son had CF so she understood the seriousness of the disease. She made sure I got plenty of rest at night and that our schedule was something I could physically handle. One of our trips to GRC stands out in my mind because my energy level was low, I felt really sick and it was painful to breathe.

It also happened to be the year the swine flu was of epidemic proportions. I went to the hotel fitness center to use the treadmill one morning like I always did. This was a very posh spa (the kind where people even whisper in the gym) and multiple personal trainers on staff. Although it was packed, there was one treadmill open. I got on and did my usual running and coughing to the point where it sounded like I was choking.

Twenty minutes later I realized the gym was noticeably empty; even the trainers were gone. Suddenly a woman appeared in front of my machine and motioned for me to take off my headset. She informed me that "I had driven all of the hotel guests away and that I had no business being there with such a terrible cough." She then told me to leave the fitness facility. I told her I understood her concern (which was hardly concern but more annoyance) but that I was not sick with the swine flu and had a lung disease no one could catch. She told me emphatically that their goal at the hotel was to provide a pleasant, relaxing experience for all their guests; she said I was a disruption and could not stay.

I was so upset that I went to find Frankie to tell him what happened. As I walked into the restaurant where I knew he'd gone for breakfast, I could smell burnt toast. Frankie loves burnt toast so I knew he was the culprit. As I approached the buffet area, I saw him waving a paper plate over the toaster to help diffuse the dark cloud of smoke rising from the toaster.

Suddenly a deafening alarm went off and lights started flashing throughout the entire hotel. It was a fire . ... no wait . . . it was Frankie's burnt toast! A recorded voice came over the loud speaker which resonated throughout the entire resort assuring the guests it was a false alarm and not to panic. Frankie and I had made quite an impression, one that the hotel staff would never forget.

~ ~ ~

Working with the Stars

After the first year of our alliance with GRC, the decision was made to have a celebrity endorse our line. The executives wanted to find someone who was genuinely a good fit and loved using Ice Elements. They sent our products to many top celebrities and many of them were interested in working with us. For various reasons, we were not very excited about many of them. They seemed too Hollywood-like and I was looking for someone who was sincere, kind and appreciated the more natural approach to beauty. We found the perfect fit in Carrie Ann Inaba.

Frankie and I knew who Carrie Ann was from having seen her on the show "In Living Color" in the early years of her professional career. As many throughout the country know, she is now one of the talent judges on "Dancing with the Stars." She is admired not only for her dancing expertise and choreography skills but for her grace and beauty as well. She is stunning. I appreciate how down-to-earth she is on the show. She appears to viewers as being an approachable celebrity and she is.

We were delighted when Coleen said that Carrie Ann used our Ice Elements and loved it. As a native of Hawaii, she felt a perfect synergy with the natural aloe vera ingredient we use. It was such an honor that she wanted to film a show together and be my co-host. I couldn't contain my excitement as Frankie and I boarded a plane in November of 2008 to meet her in Los Angeles.

She was much taller than I expected and had on some of the best-looking boots I had ever seen. She looked so trendy and hip while I was dressed like I was going to a library meeting. As you would expect, she was so gracious and complimentary. We talked and laughed for hours.

Some of the conversation was business-related but we were all so comfortable with one another that much of it was spent sharing pieces of our personal lives.

I tried to suppress my cough as much as possible but I realized if we were to work together, she needed to know I didn't have a permanent cold. So I told her about my disease. She was very understanding, sympathetic and went out of her way to make me feel comfortable. At the end of our meeting, she was definitely on board in working with us. We exchanged personal phone numbers and hugged goodbye. This was an amazing experience; we were now friends with Carrie Ann Inaba! Filming was set to start in the spring of 2009 and there was so much work to be done in the meantime.

~ ~ ~

"OK UK"

Things were now in full gear with GRC in making an infomercial. We were warned that it would take time because it was a very involved process. This turned out to be true. There were so many people involved including the script writers, set designers, wardrobe planners, models and media buyers, all the way down to the guys who sprayed the plants on the set to make them glisten during filming. While we knew we were making progress, Frankie and I were getting antsy for things to happen more quickly. We were an established brand with a proven track record and realized we had to continue additional marketing opportunities while the GRC project was coming together.

In February of 2009 we met an agent for a live TV station in the UK. It was similar to HSN and many of the HSN vendors also sold there. We eventually came to an agreement to appear on their station live and launch our 2 Minute Miracle Gel. This meant an exhausting and grueling flight we dreaded. In April we were on a plane bound for the United Kingdom. I had packed so much luggage that it looked like I was leaving the United States forever. (I think we paid more in overweight fees than we did for my ticket.) One suitcase alone contained my nebulizer machine and medicines which needed to stay packed in dry ice; in addition to that I took 20 pairs of shoes just in case! When we boarded, I was told it was best to eat dinner and then take half of a sleeping pill in order to rest. That was my plan. What I didn't anticipate was Frankie going on 'cloud duty' the entire plane ride. I knew he was a nervous flyer but I didn't realize it was to this terrified extent. He stared out the window for seven straight hours giving me play-by-play updates on all upcoming clouds, potential rain showers and the coordinates of all other planes in the vicinity. He rested his hand on my leg and it never moved. Occasionally I had to relocate it slightly because his sweaty palm was soaking my jeans. I was so worried about him that I never slept either.

The day after we arrived, we headed to the station for our introduction and program planning. The following morning we launched live on a morning show at 8 o'clock. By our second show at noon, sales were flying; while on air, the owner of the station called the producer who then notified the host (in her earpiece) that we had just set a nine-year record for the station with the premiere of our skin care line. I was on such a high that adrenaline kept my fatigue at bay. I knew, however, the stress of the flight and performing well on the shows would eventually catch up with me and it did when we returned home. As anticipated, I came down with a horrible cold which then turned into my usual sinus infection and secondary lung infection. I was put on oral antibiotics but after not responding well, I had to go back on IV's.

The station was so excited about our success that we were awarded a future "Pick of the Day." This is only given to companies that can generate a large amount of sales in 24 hours. It was a rather unique situation to have received this after one visit. We were so excited until we realized it meant traveling to the UK again. This was no longer an option. Frankie would never let me fly that far again and I couldn't bear the thought of his panic attacks.

We decided to hire a gal we knew well through HSN as our on-air spokesperson. The station agreed to this arrangement. Although sales went fairly well, it wasn't the same as doing our own show. We sent her back a few more times to sell the remaining inventory there but then had to terminate our relationship with the station. It was unfortunate because we loved being able to share our products internationally but unless we could do it ourselves, it wasn't worth the time and expense.

~ ~ ~

The Show Must Go On

The next few months flew by and GRC kept us busy in preparation for our infomercial shoot. One large segment of the show was filmed in Florida at the beautiful gulf-side resort

Marriott Spa on Marco Island. We also filmed segments in Fiddler's Creek which has such magnificent surroundings and gorgeous properties that provided the perfect backdrop for our show. Between the two locations it took four full days of shooting. It was absolutely wild to see all the production trucks, set designers and lighting crews even on the beach in full daylight and sunshine. There were nearly 50 people who needed to be present to film what may have amounted to only 10 minutes of the entire show. Once this segment was complete we would be off to California for the balance of the shoot.

My health is so sensitive to any change in routine that I always feel the foreboding presence of dark clouds hovering above me. There are so many times when I should be embracing and celebrating the moment but in the back of my mind I worry that I am one bad cold away from never recovering. I was so determined to be as healthy as possible when we filmed our main segment in LA with Carrie Ann because I wanted to be at a peak performance level. Scheduling a shooting time was a challenge because she was working on "Dancing with the Stars" which was in progress. Fortunately there were two days in July when everyone could meet. Frankie and I would have to be in LA at least four days prior to the shoot and stay a few days afterwards.

Our shoot was set for July so we decided to take another road trip and enjoy the beautiful drive to Los Angeles. Besides the anticipation of our shoot, I was just as excited about the chance for the two of us to be alone. The next few weeks were glorious; Frankie had planned a beautiful trip that would get us to San Francisco by July 13th to celebrate my birthday. We had to be in Orange County for the filming on the 17th.

At 3 a.m. on July 12th, I was awakened with excruciating pain in my side. It was so intense I had trouble breathing as perspiration dripped from my body. I tried getting up to walk it off but I couldn't stand because I was dizzy. It was so early that I didn't want to wake Frankie, even though I knew he would be mad if I didn't. By 5:30 the pain had seized control of me; we needed to find a hospital immediately. Here we were in a small town about three hours outside of San Francisco and the only thing that kept running through my mind was that we had to film in five days; so whatever type of flu I had needed to be gone quickly. I didn't have time to be sick.

After being admitted to the emergency room, the scans indicated that my appendix needed to be removed immediately. I couldn't believe it. Appendicitis was the last thing I expected. Frankie immediately drew signs warning everyone about my allergy to preservatives in saline. When we met my surgeon, he was very sympathetic and mindful that any surgery posed some degree of risk to my lungs due to my disease. I was worried more about developing a secondary lung infection from the procedure. As the anesthesiologist assured me he would watch my oxygen level closely, I drifted off without hearing the end of his sentence.

I came out of recovery at 4 p.m. and was kept overnight to monitor my lungs. I was released the next morning at 11 a.m. and we drove to San Francisco. For my birthday, Mom and Dad surprised us and sent flowers, dinner and dessert to our hotel room. I was still feeling a little weak and it hurt so badly to walk. It felt like knives were piercing through me as I buttoned my jeans. The next day I summoned the strength to do a little sight-seeing. We left San Francisco on the 15th and met our entire crew and Carrie Ann. We began filming on the 17th as planned. I made Frankie swear not to tell anyone about my surgery. I knew they would worry and tell me to take it easy; so we told no one.

The three days of shooting seemed surreal. Mom and Dad flew out to meet us so they could watch the filming, meet Carrie Ann and enjoy the entire experience. Frankie and I were treated like stars. I had my own dressing room and a luxurious trailer with my name on the door that was next to Carrie Ann's trailer. A crew member was assigned to make sure I had everything I needed at all times. Frankie sat with the production crew and although they were professionals at filming a production of this magnitude, they trusted many of his suggestions based on what he knew works for us on live TV. Carrie Ann sought our opinions on what to wear and I asked her opinion what to wear as well. Once our hair and makeup was done, the filming began. None of it was scripted and we had so much fun working together.

I am used to live TV where there are no "do overs." Filming is quite different because there are wardrobe changes, lighting changes, set changes and plenty of "do overs." We worked 10-12 hours daily for three days. I took breaks and went to the trailer to cough and try to clear my lungs so I didn't sound hoarse during the filming. I also had Frankie do percussions on my back. At the end of the successful shoot, we were all exhausted and went to dinner to celebrate. Frankie and I felt so close to Carrie Ann; we were drawn in by her sincerity and positive energy. We were sorry when the filming was over but promised to stay in touch and celebrate once we officially launched our project.

Frankie and I then had two more days of shooting at a mansion located high above the hill tops near Dana Point. At this point I was beginning to feel sick and was having pain in my lungs. We told our closest friends at GRC about my surgery and as expected, they were upset we didn't tell them sooner. Frankie and I made a trip to the local hospital and x-rays revealed I had pleurisy and some concentrated areas of congestion in my lungs. Once I was put on strong oral antibiotics, we were on our way. I felt better within a few days. It was time for us to get back on the road and start our long but satisfying journey home. We had so much to tell our family and friends.

~ ~ ~

My Initial Obsession with Abscessus

You hear the saying "stress kills" but I really am not sure I ever believed that until we began our infomercial endeavor. Although on the surface it appeared that the project was moving forward, in reality it was moving forward at a snail's pace. The long hours of planning, writing, filming, traveling and stalls in the project were really starting to take a toll on me physically. Frankie was affected too. I could see it in his face and hear it in his words. We felt like we were so close to something big but yet we couldn't quite get there.

When I say 'big' I don't mean financially rewarding as much as I mean gratifying. We wanted that sense of satisfaction in knowing we had taken something from the ground up and reached the pinnacle of our potential. Our infomercial with GRC would represent that. Despite working as hard as possible, it seemed like our efforts weren't making a difference in the painfully slow pace of the big business world. We didn't want to waste our efforts and pursue too many endeavors at once if we were to launch our infomercial, but if it didn't happen soon we realized we needed a back-up plan to grow our business outside of HSN. What exacerbated our frustrations even more was never getting answers from anyone.

I have always believed it's harder on the loved one of someone with a disease than it is on the person living with it. When you have an illness, you know exactly what you are feeling and thinking. You know your limits (even though you may ignore them). There is no guessing. But those who love you constantly have to worry how you're feeling, what you are thinking, if you are pushing yourself too much and if the demands in life are too great.

I know this is what tormented Frankie. He was so concerned about my well-being and feared what the responsibility and stress of our business was doing to me. It was horrible for him and this is what upset me. We were equally frustrated as we doubted how long we could handle this infomercial project. We talked daily in questioning whether it was worth it; more times than not we concluded that we needed to give it another month to know. A month would come and go and progress remained slow which led to more frustration and stress.

In January of 2010 I got a very bad sinus infection which affected my vocal cords. As a result, I lost my voice completely. I was barely able to eke out a whisper. This had happened to me in the past but I returned to normal after a week or two of antibiotics. This time was different. My vocal chords were traumatized because I had developed cysts which prohibited me from producing any sound. My greatest fear was that I wouldn't be able to continue doing our live HSN shows. We had six shows coming up soon so I had some time to recover. You never realize how much of your personality and joy in life is tied to your voice until you lose it.

Frankie would joke that it was a husband's dream to have a wife with no voice but deep down he was scared and angry. We developed 'our whistle' that I used to acknowledge or answer any questions he had that required a "yes" response. We also used it to help locate me in a crowded area if we were separated. (This is still our signature whistle today.) My friend, Sandra, took me out to dinner and brought a notebook in order for us to communicate. My friends at the gym invented a made-up sign language so I didn't feel like I had to talk. In spite of everyone's caring efforts to help me, I began to feel isolated from life.

I had to start voice lessons twice a week in order to re-train my voice. My ear, nose and throat specialist (ENT) and I talked about the possibility of surgery but he feared I might lose my voice permanently. He ordered a CT scan during this ordeal which indicated that my sinuses were in desperate need of another surgery which was contributing to lung infections. This bacteria growing within me was a stubborn one that didn't respond to oral antibiotics. The best option was to begin a round of IV antibiotics. The plan was to stay on them for 10-14 days to see if there was any improvement.

At the same time my lungs were really bothering me. I had more congestion and an overall tenderness when I breathed. I had a wonderful rapport with my CF doctor and felt comfortable calling or emailing him with any questions regarding my health. I called him and explained my sinus and lung issues. He told me that he didn't want to discuss things over the phone so perhaps I should come to his office to "discuss a few new developments with my health." Mom and Dad were in town visiting us at the time and we were all enjoying the day at an outdoor art fair in a beautiful park in downtown Naples. The sun was out and the temperature was perfect. What a wonderful day! Frankie and Dad had had their fill of walking around oohing and ahhing at everything and had gone to get a cup of coffee. The primary concern of my parents has always been my health and I wanted to spare them any discouraging news. So instead of their traveling three hours with us for the doctor's appointment, I asked for more details over the phone. I could tell by the tone of his voice that it was something serious.

He said my most recent culture had grown a bacteria called 'mycobacterium abscessus' which can cause a chronic lung infection and is something that is becoming more prevalent in those with CF. It is a bacteria that can cause irreparable lung damage and it's almost impossible to eradicate as it's resistant to most antibiotics-even IV antibiotics. He explained that they don't treat it in every case because the treatments are so hard on your body and other organs; the protocol would possibly mean one year on IV antibiotics through a porta-cath which would be surgically placed in my upper chest wall.

He emphasized that it eventually becomes a "quality of life" issue. My doctor was always the type to comfort me. Knowing he was worried, concerned me even more. Mom stood next to me as I listened intently; she read my sad expression. As I talked, she looked up the information and research on her Blackberry. She couldn't disguise her sadness either. We tried to rally one another by saying everything would be okay but we knew this diagnosis would possibly change the rest of my life. As we went to tell Frankie and Dad what had taken us so long while they were cooling their heels, we now knew that decisions would have to be made whether to have the treatment or not. Little did I know that this brutal diagnosis would haunt me forever.

~ ~ ~

Silent Tears

There are some days which are few and far between when I have a good cry. I wait until Frankie is gone or I pretend I'm doing laundry in the other room. Then I cry but only for a minute or so.

These aren't tears of pain or self-pity but more of frustration. Today was like that. Maybe it was just a culmination of this past week with the diagnosis of having abscessus that almost trumped my CF diagnosis. I have lived with CF my entire life and I know it. I am not afraid of it. I feel like I have emotional control over it. Now I'm facing a new unknown and I feel scared and depressed.

It is no secret that my CF alone will cause my lung functions and health to decline as I get older. So it is going to happen regardless. The question now becomes how much faster will I decline with the abscessus? This bacteria has only recently become prevalent in CF patients but it is still a relatively new finding and treatments are still in the experimental phase. There are not many proven ways to totally eradicate it. At some point a life-altering decision will have to be made whether to treat it or wait. The confusion, frustration and lack of definitive information can be overwhelming. So tonight I waited until Frankie went to pick up dinner and I shed my silent tears. I feel better now.

~ ~ ~

The Pillar of Strength

Frankie, it's been awhile since I've emailed you for information in the book. After reading Shelly's emotional words about the silent tears she cries, I find myself thinking of you and the silent tears you cry. You are Shelly's pillar of strength and security with every breath she takes. How do you remain so strong when your heart aches for her?

Beth

~ ~ ~

Other Silent Tears

Beth, this is Frankie. As you can tell from what Shelly just shared, the diagnosis of the abscessus bacteria has been tough on both of us. I know she's been crying many silent tears. She thinks I don't realize it from time to time but I do. There is a sadness in her eyes that only I can see and feel.

My job is to be strong, make her smile and help take her mind off her terrible disease. When I think of where Shelly is right now, I don't get too sad because that won't help her. Instead I say, "Today I have Shelly and let's celebrate life." We're all going to die someday; there are no guarantees any of us will even outlive Shelly. I try desperately to live for the moment and not think of the inevitable. If I outlive Shelly, I won't ever look back and think I should have loved her more or we should have enjoyed life more. That isn't possible because I couldn't love her and our beautiful life together more.

They say everyone in life is replaceable. Not my Shelly. My biggest concern is dying before she does because she adores and cherishes me like no other. If I weren't by her side, her health would decline, she would be devastated and could possibly give up to some degree. I hate thinking about this and that's why I pray that I live just as long as Shelly. While we have each other, there is no giving up ever.

~ ~ ~

Falling Apart Slowly

Dear Beth,

When we started my story, I promised to share the good, the bad and the ugly. I forgot to tell you about 'the unexpected' I would also need to share. After more than two weeks of being on IV antibiotics, my sinus infection was better and my lung pain was starting to decrease. However, I started having pain in my teeth. My front teeth became very sensitive and so did a few of my side upper and lower teeth. Frankie and I saw our dentist and upon examining my x-rays, she suggested I see an endodontist for root canals. We set up an appointment, met with the endodontist and heard more bad news. Although he could do root canals on multiple teeth, that would not solve the problem. It appeared that some type of infection had infiltrated the bones of the teeth and had split the roots. A few of my teeth couldn't be saved.

Frankie looked at me with the saddest eyes I have ever seen and held my hand as I asked more questions. The dentist presented my options which included implants or a bridge and told me the entire process would take approximately four months to complete. I make my living on TV and although I am not a vain woman, I am in a business that depends on vanity. As much as I hated the fact, I had to deal with this and I was equally fixated on how much I would have to spend. My philosophy has always been if I can't eat it or wear it, I don't want to buy it.

In the midst of all of this health trauma, I also started having tremendous abdominal pain. I was almost too embarrassed to tell Frankie or anyone because it was starting to seem ridiculous. Our days were spent going from one doctor to another and having one test after another. When an ultra sound showed I would need abdominal surgery, my lung doctor and I talked about this at length. Since my lungs were now healthier due to the IV meds I had recently finished, we decided it would be a good time to get all of the health-related surgeries done throughout the month.

In March I had extensive mouth surgery, sinus surgery and abdominal surgery. I was forced to slow down and stop talking while I recovered. This gave my vocal cords time to heal and that was one of my greatest priorities since my next HSN show was quickly approaching. With all my surgeries and illnesses slowly becoming a distant memory, I was able to get back on track with my life. We were now working long hours to launch A new skin care line for An international company who had hired us to consult and formulate a full range of skin care for them. We were doing this while also working on the eventual launch of our infomercial project with GRC. Even though I was now on the mend, Frankie and I were still feeling a tremendous amount of pressure. The infomercial project stressed us out the most. I think it was the result of having so little control over the process and having a successful test meant so much to our future.

We realized that the year had flown by so quickly and it would soon be time for our annual road trip somewhere. As much as we love planning our trips, we have more fun not planning them and winging it as we go. Most people would find this somewhat unsettling but there is something about the feeling of freedom and adventure that we both relish.

One time when we needed to fly to LA for one of our shoots, we decided to fly there, rent a car and drive back home making many stops along the way. At the end of our shoot, Carrie Ann, the crew and all of our friends at GRC were saying their goodbyes and they asked what time our flight was leaving. We said we didn't book a flight because we were going to drive. Everyone stared at us with an expression of "Huh? Are you nuts?" They thought we were even crazier when they asked where we would be stopping and we said, "We have no plans. We just need to be back home within a month." Only a few voiced the sentiments that many were thinking:

"What a great way to live life!" and it was.

~ ~ ~

Detour

It was time to start thinking about our trip so Frankie and I spent a few weeks studying the oversized map of the U.S. that covers one of our office walls. I was focused on traveling through the Midwest and then over to the East Coast. I had never been to Rhode Island to see where he grew up and I wanted to meet the rest of his family who lived there. He was more determined to travel to the West Coast. He thought it would be a nice idea to have dinner in Las Vegas at our favorite spot overlooking the fountains at Olives restaurant in the Bellagio. I loved the idea because that was such a special place for both of us.

With our car packed to the gills, we headed out the first part of June. Per usual, I worked on the laptop while Frankie drove and chewed his gum. We planned and re-planned our life and brainstormed about 20 other business ventures we could start. We reached the same conclusion each time. We didn't have the time or want the stress. After being on the road for only one week, I already felt rejuvenated. One evening around 5 o'clock, we decided to stop in a small town in Alabama that was a good resting place close to the highway. We thought we could have an early dinner, get some rest and then head out in the morning to arrive in Memphis the following day.

After dinner we headed back to our lodging when I suddenly felt a hot flush come over me followed by pain shooting into my shoulder. I didn't say anything at first but the pain became more intense. I looked to my left and we just happened to be passing what looked like a state- of-the-art hospital. I finally said, "I think I may be having a heart attack, but I'm not sure. Could you pull into the hospital?" Frankie immediately jerked the car to the left and sped to the emergency room. I was not yet sold on the idea of going in because I wasn't sure if I needed help. If it turned out that nothing was wrong, we would have wasted so many hours. We had tickets to see the play "Chicago" in Memphis the following day and I didn't want to miss it.

I said, "Let's sit in the emergency room waiting area to see if I am having a heart attack. If I don't, we can leave." He was adamant we were going to check in as we sat in the waiting area loudly discussing my pending heart attack. The woman at the check-in desk kept looking up and asking if she could help. I assured her that IF I were having a heart attack, I would probably know in a few more minutes and then we would be happy to register. She gave me a blank stare with her eyebrows raised into her hairline. Frankie was getting more upset with me for being so stubborn and decided to call for back-up help. He went right to the top and called Mom. Once he explained the situation, she demanded I check in or she would personally drive there herself. That threat was enough to make me take action.

When you say you are having a possible heart attack, you move right to the front of any emergency room waiting line. After hours and hours of tests and blood work, the doctor told me my pancreas was inflamed and I had pancreatitis. My enzymes were nearly triple what they should be. He also thought he saw a little pneumonia or area of congestion in my left lower lung. I couldn't believe it because I was feeling so good. I had been on a very heavy course of oral antibiotics over the last two months (trying to fight the abscessus bacteria) and the doctor concluded that perhaps it was antibiotic-induced pancreatitis. I had lost a little weight unintentionally over the last few months due to the side effects of my medicine so I was trying hard to gain back a few pounds by eating pizza, hot dogs and fried foods my body couldn't tolerate. The doctor suspected this had also exacerbated the problem. Although a large majority of CF patients have pancreatic problems, I have a mutation of the disease which doesn't involve the pancreas. It was always thought that if I didn't have the issue as a child, I would never have the issue as an adult. This later proved to be wrong.

As planned and with the doctor's approval, we headed out the next morning. I was immediately barraged with phone calls from my family. Although Mom and Dad knew how much it meant to me to stop in Memphis, they wanted us in Missouri as soon as possible. Mindy, a highly skilled nurse, called and told me what to do and what not to do and strongly encouraged me to go directly to Kansas City where I could be seen by some of the best medical specialists she knew. Lori was so worried she offered to fly to Kansas City to meet me if I needed her there.

Deep down, I knew my family was right but I was torn emotionally. So was Frankie because he knew how important our trip was to me; he also realized I would get the best care if I went to Mom and Dad's. We decided to stay, go to the play and then see how I felt the next day. I was still feeling so sick and weak and the doctor's parting orders were to go on a liquid diet for the most part which meant clear liquids, no solids and no fats. I was so discouraged but I took his orders seriously.

I felt even worse the next day and almost too weak to travel. I wanted to be in the hospital so we headed to Kansas City. It was now the last part of June and my birthday was only a few weeks away. We had planned to be in Vegas by my birthday so I needed to get better quickly. As we pulled up to Mom and Dad's house, I felt tremendous relief. I was home and as Frankie always says, "There is nothing that can replace your mother's love and care, Shelly." This was so true.

By now I was running a fever, had tremendous abdominal pain and lung pain that was intensified with every labored breath. In typical Mom fashion, she had anticipated this moment so plans were already in place for me to go right to the hospital, be admitted and examined by a leading internist, pulmonologist and other top medical specialists. There were so many people in and out of my room I was getting confused; I talked about my lungs to the pancreas guy and talked about my pancreas to the floor sweeper.

After a battery of tests and a pain killer (which I don't like to ever take) it was determined that my pancreas enzymes were still very high, I had pneumonia and was feeling pleurisy symptoms due to the residual inflammation. I would need a course of IV antibiotics and couldn't leave the hospital for at least five days or more. I was even more depressed. We had so many exciting things planned for vacation and my birthday and here I was sick again in the hospital. I could tell by the doctors' discussions that this was serious and I couldn't take my treatments lightly. My pancreas issue posed a significant problem that necessitated remaining on a liquid diet for many days and possibly weeks. The issue of my weight loss had to be addressed as well. I looked very thin, frail and sickly. I think this was one of the few times where I felt truly scared. Breathing incurred intense pain, it hurt to sleep and I felt drained emotionally and physically. I just wanted to lie in bed which was so atypical of me. Mindy was so worried about my weight loss that she brought cases of Ensure and high calorie drinks but I had little interest in even swallowing them because it took too much energy.

One evening when my therapist was performing a chest percussion treatment, we talked about Vegas. I told her we were going there for my birthday (which was now in eight days) and she remarked she was going there to be married. She said she had put it off for years because of the hassle but she and her fiance' were finally going to do it. I told her how much I loved my boyfriend, that we'd been together for nine years and were always too busy to plan a wedding. Our conversation made me stop and think about those things in life that matter most.

I called Frankie at Mom's house and told him I'd like to get married and if we kept waiting for the right time, it might be too late. I wanted to be his wife; there was no one I could ever love more. He was silent until I finished and said, "That's a great idea. Let's plan it." The fact that I was sick at the time made us both realize that life is short and fragile and we needed to live for today.

He thought we should ask Mom and Dad to be our witnesses. I loved the idea but felt badly my sisters wouldn't be there. I also wanted my extended family and close friends to witness this special moment but didn't want to inconvenience everyone by asking them to make travel plans on such short notice. We decided to explain to everyone our desire to marry and asked for their blessings to go on without them. They were all gracious and happy for us. My Aunt Marlene said she would throw a big wedding party after we returned. It was settled. I would become Mrs. Tedesco in a few weeks. I was motivated to get well immediately.

~ ~ ~

The Preparation

I had now been in the hospital five days. After our decision to get married, there was suddenly so much to be done. Yet here I was stuck in the hospital. Frankie had approached Mom and Dad about coming to Vegas for my birthday dinner and then they could stay to be witnesses at our wedding. Of course, all these plans were going to be on hold if the doctors didn't release me. I was feeling much better and my lung pain had finally started to subside. Mom was worried that perhaps the drive to Vegas would be too much for me but flying would be much worse; my immune system was already weakened and I'd be more susceptible to germs.

We devised a plan. If I was released by the 9th, we could buy wedding rings and outfits, leave on the 10th and arrive on the 12th. Then we would have one full day to celebrate my birthday and the surprise Frankie had planned for me. All I knew was that it included dinner at Bellagio's. As much as I love a surprise, I was hoping whatever he'd planned didn't require much energy on my part. Although he had put so much time into organizing things, he assured me if for some reason I wasn't released from the hospital or if I couldn't handle the trip, we'd do it another time. I was determined, however, to go.

On the morning of the 9th the doctors came in and said they were waiting for my lab work to determine if my picc line could be removed and if they could release me on heavy oral antibiotics for my lungs and pancreatic enzymes for my pancreas. It all boiled down to results from one test that seemed to be taking forever. I was already packed, showered and ready to go so I hoped my blood work would cooperate. At 11 o'clock the doctor released me and by 2 o'clock Mom and I were shopping.

I wasn't looking for a traditional wedding dress so she set a few aside the day before she thought I'd like. She was dead on accurate. I actually bought one dress for my birthday dinner (Mom thought the one I brought was a bit lackluster) and a steel gray off-the- shoulder silk dress for the wedding. We then scurried to a fine men's clothing store and found a suit for Frankie. It was a beautiful deeper gray which complimented my dress. He looked so handsome when he tried on his suit that I couldn't wait to marry this man I loved. The suit needed altering so they said we could pick it up early the next morning before we headed out.

The next mission was buying wedding rings. In anticipation of my release, Mom had also gone to her jeweler a few days prior and described what I was looking for in a ring. I wanted a simple band with a few diamonds around it similar to an eternity ring. When the jeweler brought out a magnificent sparkling band that was wrapped with two rows of diamonds, Frankie fell in love with it right away. I did too but it was much more than I needed. After an hour of trying on every other ring in the store, I agreed to get the stunning band Frankie loved. The jeweler said he would have it sized to fit me by a custom jeweler in New York and sent to Vegas in time for our wedding. Frankie picked out a band which, of course, was simple. When he tried it on I thought he looked even more attractive.

We returned to Mom and Dad's and packed to leave the next morning. It had been a whirlwind but we got everything done. I commented how shocked I was that everything fell into place so easily. It wasn't until later that I found out this was no coincidence at all.

~ ~ ~

The Surprise

We arrived in Vegas on the afternoon of the 12th and immediately applied for a marriage license. Mom said she had already found a little place where we could get married and lined up a rabbi to officiate. (She said she could fill me in on these details later.) Frankie was acting a little strange; he simply wasn't himself. He not only seemed nervous and scatter-brained but kept disappearing as well. He repeatedly went to the front desk to schedule some kind of tour.

There was a waiting list and I was secretly hoping we couldn't go. The thought of touring Vegas in 109 degree heat all day and then going to dinner later that night would be too much. He was also on the phone a lot and whenever he took a call, he walked away. I'm used to his pacing when he's on the phone; it's a habit. But he was actually walking away during his calls.

He finally informed me that part of his plans for the following day had fallen through so instead he'd booked a full day at the spa for us from 9 a.m. to 4 p.m. Then we'd shower and have a lovely dinner with Mom and Dad. I couldn't comprehend spending seven hours at the spa which sounded like torture. How could we relax for seven hours? Normally Frankie would despise something like this but he was so excited about his upcoming body wrap and pedicure. This was so out of character for him. Did I really know this man I was marrying?

When I saw the prices of staying at the Bellagio and added the cost of our marathon day at the spa, I calculated it to be over our mortgage payment. I didn't want to seem ungrateful for all he'd done so I acted equally excited. If this wasn't already perplexing, he took it a step further and rented an environmental room where we could relax, meditate, drink juice and smell some natural herbs! I finally had to speak up and say, "Frankie, they're trying to oversell us! WHY would we need to pay an additional $100 to relax in a room for an hour after already relaxing for seven hours? He insisted this was something he wanted and could I do it for him? I had no choice but to agree.

I did my early morning work-out on my birthday although I was interrupted by family members and friends calling to say "Happy Birthday!" When I spoke to my sisters and a few of my closest friends, I felt a pang of sadness that I was celebrating my birthday and wedding without them. Mindy and Lori assured me that their thoughts and good wishes were with me.

But it just wouldn't be the same without my sisters.

Frankie was acting a little odd and had nervous energy. I didn't know how he would ever relax for our spa retreat. He was even a little bossy which is not his style. He was adamant about the path we should take through the hotel to the spa. He insisted that our lunch be served in the back spa area and not in their spa dining area where people can walk by and look in. He also told me that if for some reason I finished a little ahead of him that I had to go right to the environmental room and not leave the area until he arrived. I figured he really wanted our day to be perfect and filled with romance and privacy.

At the conclusion of our spa extravaganza, I couldn't get out of there quickly enough. I was exhausted from over relaxing (if that is possible). But we still had one more hour booked in the environmental room to sit, meditate and smell herbs. I did that for about fifteen minutes and then begged Frankie to forfeit the remaining time. He finally compromised. He agreed to leave if we could take the long way around the hotel to our room. He thought it would be invigorating to take a walk around the outside perimeter of the expansive hotel property. I didn't think a 30-minute walk in 112 degree heat would invigorate me but I was so ready to simply see some natural light that I agreed to it.

We finally got back to our room to shower and get ready. Normally when we plan to go somewhere, I'm the one who drives Frankie crazy with planning our departure time down to the second. I even have it timed down to the second I want to be walking out the door. But this time, he was the one driving me crazy. He told me we had to leave the room and be walking down the hall toward dinner at exactly 6:45. As we were ready to depart, he suddenly had a stomach ache and had to use the bathroom. After 10 minutes, he emerged. We started to head out the door again and his phone rang. As he was answering it he ran back into the bathroom and hollered out, "My stomach hurts again. It's just my brother. I'll talk to him while I'm in here." Five minutes later I heard the hair dryer going full speed. What in the world was he doing? I yelled in to see if he was okay and he yelled back that he spilled water on the front of his shirt and was going to blow dry it quickly. He was acting so odd but I dismissed it as pre-wedding jitters.

Finally he was out of the bathroom and then spent another 15 minutes on his hair. I was starting to get a little annoyed because I didn't want to miss the sunset. At 7:30 we finally left our room and headed over to Olives. I had asked Frankie to bring our video camera so we could video the fountains and our evening with Mom and Dad. As we walked in the front of Olives, he turned on the camera and began commentating as we walked through the bar towards the beautiful glass double doors which lead to the balcony. As I approached the doors, I saw Mom and Dad already seated. I heard Frankie continuing to talk to the camera but I was not listening to what he was saying. I was more confused because it looked like Mom and Dad were seated with someone else. I merely thought it was typical of them making friends with a stranger.

As two doormen opened up both glass doors at the same time, we had a wide panoramic view of the balcony. Wait a minute. Mom and Dad were sitting with my Aunt Marlene. I thought "How wild that she is here in Vegas, too! Wow, she was with my cousins, Jody and Barbara, who lived nearby. She must have been visiting them." Then I glanced over and saw Frankie's brother, Mike, and his wife, Theresa. Why were they here when Mike had to work? As I walked onto the balcony I saw my sister, Mindy. She couldn't be here! I talked to her earlier in the day and she was at work. And wait, Lori and her husband, Mike, were here too and I just saw them two days ago as we passed through Sante Fe. Even my dear friends Coco and Keith were here and they never travel without their precious son, Zachary, who is autistic and deaf. Uncle Gary and Aunt Patti were there and he was going through radiation on his throat and couldn't travel.

It was all happening so fast and my mind was trying to make sense of what I was seeing. Then suddenly I heard a loud roar from everyone on the balcony . . . "Surprise!!!" When I saw Linda, Dale and Coleen, everything made sense. This was a surprise party for ME. I was so shocked that I started sobbing and couldn't catch my breath. Mindy hurried over in the event she had to resuscitate me. I couldn't stop crying and I couldn't utter any words except, "Oh my God." It took a good fifteen minutes to identify everyone who was there to celebrate.

Then I realized I was getting married the next day and although many of my cousins, niece, nephews and close friends weren't there, I felt blessed to have so many there I loved. I started putting the pieces together as more details of the plan were divulged. The reason we had to spend an entire day in the spa was that Frankie had to keep me out of our hotel and occupied so everyone could get checked in without being seen. The reason he spent so much time in the bathroom when it was time to leave for dinner was that his brother was delayed and needed to give Frankie updated information.

Everyone had a secret story to tell and what I found most touching (and surprising to say the least) was that this plan started back in April with Frankie asking my parents' permission to marry; this was followed by an email from him to everyone explaining his idea to give me a birthday surprise and a wedding I would never forget. Mom asked, "Frankie, are you sure she will say 'yes' before we start planning this?"

While I thought I was busy helping to pull together last minute details for our wedding (getting a dress, a ring, a suit etc), he and Mom had been busy at work for months planning and coordinating everything. None of it was my idea like I originally thought. He had kept it a secret for all these months. I told him I could only imagine how torn he must have been when I was hospitalized and there was a chance we would have to call this off. He assured me the only thing on his mind was my getting better and nothing else mattered at that time.

As the sun began to set and the noise of the crowd was silenced by the sound of the majestic fountains dancing to "our song," we were both overcome with emotion. Tears welled up in our eyes and we embraced each other tightly. I whispered to him that although I didn't tell him at the time, my last hospital bout scared me. It made me realize how much I loved him and that I desperately wanted to spend the rest of my life (however long it would be) as Mrs. Tedesco. He said he felt the same way and wanted to call me his wife forever. At that moment, I knew I was marrying the man who I had dreamed about marrying one day. Frankie was that caring, funny, kind, sensitive and perfect man just like my Dad.

~ ~ ~

"I Do"

Although I had arrived in Las Vegas only two days prior, a little too thin, frail and weak, I felt great. There was such an adrenaline high from all the excitement that I forgot about being sick.

With all of the focus on my birthday party, it occurred to me I didn't know anything about our wedding plans. Usually the bride carries the burden of worry but in this case I only had to be dressed and ready. Mom and my cousin Barbara (who lives in Vegas and helped with the plans) had all the worrying to do regarding our wedding ceremony and celebration.

The ceremony and lunch were held at the beautiful Bali Hai Golf Club which made the perfect setting with palm trees, waterfalls and lush floral landscaping. Although Frankie is not Jewish, he was comfortable with having a reformed Rabbi perform our ceremony which included the traditions of having a wedding canopy and breaking a glass at the end of the ceremony. We thought it was fascinating to learn that our rabbi had been close friends with Jerry Lewis. He shared a few great stories about that part of his life as we discussed the flow of our ceremony. By then, all the guests had arrived and were seated outside on the patio area overlooking the golf course and a beautiful waterfall in the background.

Even though the rabbi only met us for an hour prior to our ceremony, he was able to capture the love and the sentiments of the moment. His words touched everyone's heart and I think because we all knew the struggles I had personally faced in the last few weeks, his words made an even greater impact. As Frankie and I stood up to exchange vows, we looked out through our teary eyes to see there was not a dry eye in the group. The service was very tender and emotional. A small oversight by the rabbi added some levity to the moment when he accidentally referred to Frankie as Mike who was the best man. You could hear a gasp in unison when he asked Mike if he would take my hand in marriage. We all got a good laugh out of that including the rabbi.

My cousin, Marc, graciously acted as our photographer and my close friend, Sandra, sang our wedding song "At Last." She sounded beautiful and the words so perfectly expressed my love for Frankie that once again I began to cry. So did everyone else. After we were pronounced husband and wife, we all retreated to a private area where an elegant lunch was served. As we ate, each guest got up to say a few special words and toast the occasion. Although it was never expressed aloud, we all privately reflected on our own lives and embraced the moment. Everyone was here to celebrate the true meaning of love between two people. Frankie and I were now husband and wife!

~ ~ ~

Two Hearts as One

Dear Beth,

I shed the same tears of joy at Shelly's wedding that I did when our daughters Mindy and Lori married the loves of their lives, too. Felicia and I couldn't have dreamed for more and feel such peace in our hearts.

Throughout the wedding ceremony, I was trying to experience it through Shelly's emotions. I hoped she saw the beautiful waterfall and surroundings as something she deserved. I did. I hoped she saw the gathering of friends and family as a loving tribute to who she is. I did. I know she saw Frankie's overwhelming (over-the-top) effort to give her a memorably happy day as testimony of his boundless love for her. So did I. After living her life under an undeserved cloud of fear and uncertainty medically, here was a defiant statement embracing the well-deserved promise of a happy future together. Finally we were all witnessing a moment of "fairness" in life that made this day even more meaningful.

Now I need to step aside and let the love of my life share her feelings.

Seymour

~ ~ ~

As a mother, Beth, one always looks back and questions "why didn't I . . . ?" Perhaps it's in the passing of time where unpleasant memories fade away, but in all honesty I feel like the only thing I've done perfectly in life is raise my three daughters into the fantastic women they are today. Their unbelievable love for each other and their Dad and me gives me the greatest joy there is in life. My love for each of them knows no bounds. Although this book is about Shelly, I can't think of her alone because of their attachments to each other.

So, on the way to the wedding the next day, Seymour and I rode with Frankie and Shelly. Mind you, every one was told it was at Cili Restaurant in the Bali Hai Golf Club and an address and directions. It was on our way that Seymour and I think Frankie got his first exhibition of wedding jitters. We had the directions, but the street names were unfamiliar; Shelly, Seymour and I knew he was heading in the wrong direction, but Frankie was determined to go the way he wanted to go . . . and the more wrong directions he took, the faster he drove. It was a side of Frankie we hadn't seen and we were thinking the thoughts all parents feel when they're delivering their daughter into the care of another man (although they had been together for so many years already). But we finally got there and while Shelly and Frankie met with the Rabbi and talked, we all gathered, had champagne and enjoyed the outdoor patio in 120 degree Las Vegas heat.

Frankie laughs today about how we must have felt on that drive to the wedding. That's one of the greatest attributes of Frankie. If he is impetuous and stubborn at a given time, he quickly realizes that perhaps he was too determined in his position and listens more openly to the other side. Too few people have that humility to apologize.

So, the beautiful wedding is taking place. I say beautiful because the look on Shelly's and Frankie's faces under the canopy said it all. Their eyes reflected the image of the other and their faces reflected the "at last" for them as their close friend, Sandra, sang that song. Everything in their past lives was gone in the minutes of the ceremony and they really felt and wanted to be man and wife. I looked at the faces of those there and everyone, to a person, had that same look on their face; joy, warmth, approval, happiness beyond description. I couldn't look at Seymour because he was crying (not unusual for him and that's one of the indications of his warmth about most everything). I felt peace! Although I had always been comfortable knowing Frankie would be by Shelly's side for all times (good and some less pleasant), I really felt this cemented their relationship and approved by family and friends when we all yelled Mazel Tov when Frankie crushed the glass under his foot at the end of the ceremony and they kissed.

Beth, you asked how I felt following the wedding, did I have any concerns that were different than usual? My answer is no. I/we always are concerned about Shelly's health, how her schedule affects her, what's the best path to follow as far as medical treatment, etc. However, we had no doubts or reservations about her being married and protected by Frankie. His love, commitment, generosity and kindness warm my heart every day. We couldn't love him more if he were our own son.

The accolades will come from others; they need not be repeated by me. I feel pain with each cough, each clearing of her throat, each time she says, "I have to be home by 9 p.m. to get in all my night treatments." However, I need only to say that the admiration she receives from others fills my heart with such pride and I agree . . . there is none like her and how privileged I am to be able to say 'I'm her mom.'

Felicia

~ ~ ~

Life Goes On

Once Frankie and I returned home, things were back to business as usual. Although we vowed to slow down in our new life together and take time to smell the roses, it was total insanity again.

Although pleased with results of the test launch of our infomercial with Guthy-Renker, three years had passed and it was time to negotiate a new contract between all parties involved. We knew this would be a lengthy process; we also knew it would take a long time to film a new infomercial which would be needed because some of the material was now outdated and doing so would cause more stress for me. Consequently, a mutual decision was made to terminate our agreement. Frankie and I knew this would be in our best interest and would give us the ability to pursue other ventures we had previously passed up due to contractual obligations. The hardest part was saying farewell to so many friends we had made in the GRC organization. We knew we would stay in touch with Coleen and Elliott who had now become our close friends.

I felt tremendous relief after this decision. I honestly believe my health took a notable decline during that three-year period due to the stress of the entire project. Frankie and I began putting together our own infomercial project; something on a smaller scale that we could control. By focusing on this, we had more time to grow our HSN business and develop additional formulas and products.

The spring of 2011 seemed to fly by and our business was growing rapidly. All was good with that part of my life. However, my visits to the CF clinic revealed that my lung volume was slowly declining. I was also having problems with more congestion and stomach (pancreas) pain. On top of this, I was losing weight. It felt strange to be in this position having been overweight in the past and consumed with dieting. Now I was on the opposite end of the spectrum. It was a rude awakening and very depressing. I used to envy thin people. When some would share their struggles to gain weight, I assumed they weren't trying hard enough.

Now I have a totally different perspective. Before I step on the scales, I actually get nervous. I say a quick prayer that I haven't lost more. I know from my research and many conversations with my doctors that abscessus can cause weight loss. I also know that as I get older and my lungs have to work harder to breathe, I will burn more calories making it even harder to gain weight. I look at old pictures of myself and wish I had my chunky arms and fat face back again.

I've had more cultures done at the CF clinic and a few revealed that I do have the abcsessus bacteria once again. The puzzling issue is that not every culture tested positive. My doctors shared with me that three successive positive cultures are needed for confirmation. However, there are also other signs they consider. My weight loss and declining pulmonary functions are a big part of the equation. During this time, my doctor, whom I had been seeing for years, was leaving his position at our CF clinic. I respected and trusted him so much. While it saddened me when Dr. Light left, I've found great comfort in the quality of care I receive from his highly skilled professional staff and my new doctors.

I am haunted daily with questions about abscessus. In search of answers, I contacted the National Jewish Hospital in Colorado to work with their infectious disease department in the hopes they would provide some insight and a specific protocol of treatment. After a few months of sending cultures, CT scan evaluations, blood work, etc, there are still no conclusive answers on my health status and even less information in knowing how to treat me. I've been told there is a difference of opinion between infectious disease doctors and pulmonary doctors who specialize in the treatment of CF, in terms of how aggressively to treat the bacteria. Honestly, it is exhausting, confusing and upsetting. The more opinions I get and the more research I do leads me to believe that perhaps doing nothing is best. My doctors have all suggested I take a wait-and-see approach. I completely trust them and know they are looking out for my best interests. So once again I've decided to stop searching for the one right answer and just enjoy life.

~ ~ ~

The Clampetts Retire

As the summer of 2011 approached, Frankie and I had a very busy four months planned. We had our HSN shows the first week in May then hoped to start phase 1 of our next "Clampett's trip." We wanted to be in Rhode Island by late June so we mapped out a great vacation that would have us on the road for six weeks seeing all the sights along the East Coast. We spent the first week in Asheville, North Carolina, where we had been many times in the past. What we didn't know is that there are over 20 spectacular waterfalls within driving distance of Asheville. Spending time together in the gorgeous outdoors was so therapeutic.

We also travelled through the mountains of the Grand Cascades in New Jersey (I never realized New Jersey had mountains), toured the battleships in Baltimore, went to Sandra's 50th birthday party in Toms River, New Jersey, and finally made our way to Rhode Island for Frankie's family reunion.

I didn't know what to expect. Frankie had always painted such a grim picture of the state where he grew up and I suppose it was due to his upbringing. Although he has happy childhood memories, they are somewhat overshadowed by the struggles he and his brothers faced in being raised by a single parent. I fell in love with Frankie's family immediately. His mother, Ellie, is quite a character; she is mighty in spite of barely standing 4' 6" tall. We developed an instant bond. I also enjoyed the time spent with his brother Mike's family (with whom I am very close), his cousins, aunt and uncles.

As an adult, Frankie has a completely new appreciation for his mother and realizes how hard she worked to provide a stable home and safe environment even when she had nothing. He showed me a few of the small apartments (not in the nicest areas of town) where he grew up which is in stark contrast to the life he leads today. I understand why he is so proud of our accomplishments.

We returned to Florida in late July to do another set of HSN shows. I felt great which was dramatically different from the previous summer trips when I returned home ill. However, my friend, Dale, was not doing well and was slowly losing his battle with cancer. We decided to do our shows, drive to St. Louis to spend time with Dale, then drive to Kansas City. Mom was having extensive back surgery and would be very limited in movement for six weeks. I desperately wanted to be there to help her. She has done so much for me in life that this was my chance to unselfishly give back. We also planned to return to St. Louis for Robyn's daughter's wedding. Her kids are like family to me and I didn't want to miss this special occasion.

We were at HSN and had one more show to do in the morning. I was in frequent touch with Linda and her kids to stay updated on Dale's condition. The following morning I got a call from her son, Matt. Dale had passed away. My knees buckled and I sat on the steps of the hotel and cried. I never got to say goodbye to my dear friend. Earlier that week I spoke to him briefly and told him to hang in there and be strong until I got there. He said, "I will do that for you Shellbell." Frankie and I immediately drove to St. Louis to pay our last respects to Dale and to give comfort to Linda. All the girls and guys from our past Beauty Source location and several other special friends attended the funeral. Together we celebrated life – just the way Dale would have wanted it.

My sister Lori and I always try to coordinate our trips back home since it is so far to travel between Santa Fe and Naples. I count the days until I can see LorLor and my darling niece, Sophia. I was so excited at the thought of being with both of my sisters again to reminisce, laugh and hug one another. Unfortunately Lori and her family had to return to Santa Fe sooner than I'd hoped so we only had two precious days all together with Mindy and her family, too.

All too soon Lori was getting ready to leave for the airport. Sophia was in the car seat and I was standing next to Frankie as he rested his hand on the back window that was partially open. Lori started the car so she could turn on the air conditioner. Out of habit, she rolled up the window and before Frankie could remove his hand, the window sliced through his middle finger down to the first knuckle. I was hysterical while he tried to calm me down. I called 911 and the operator said my husband sounded fine in the background but it was my hysteria she was worried about more.

Mom was trying to keep things calm so Sophia wouldn't be traumatized. Lori didn't want to leave but Mom didn't want Sophia there when the ambulance came so we bid them goodbye. Although it seemed like hours until they arrived, Frankie was quickly transported to the hospital with Mom and me following closely behind with Frankie's severed finger on ice in a plastic bag. Poor Lori was in shock and guilt-ridden, so it only made things worse when we learned the doctors couldn't reattach his finger. Frankie felt worse for Lori than he did for himself. This accident gave me another insight into his strength. His only emotional moment was when the bandage was removed for the first time. Mindy's neighbor is a surgeon and offered to help Frankie with the changing of the dressing until he got used to it. Thereafter Frankie always says it could have been worse and uses it as a conversation piece.

The entire trip was wearing me down; the emotional stress of our HSN shows, Dale's funeral and now Frankie's accident was catching up with me. A few days later I began to feel sick, started coughing up more blood and felt increasing lung pain with every breath I took. It was clear to everyone we wouldn't be able to stay for Robyn's daughter's wedding or Mom's surgery. Upon returning home, I was immediately admitted to the hospital for two weeks of IV antibiotics and more therapy. I started to think it may be time for the Clampetts to retire.

~ ~ ~

The Runner-up

"Hey Beth! It's Shelly. I'm almost afraid to ask how your day has gone because I know you were working on the book way too late last night."

"I'm energized, Lady! I can't wait to include the material you sent yesterday. The readers are going to enjoy the 'Crazy in Love' entry. It's reminded me of a very long phone conversation we had when we were about two months into the book."

"I don't think we've ever had a short conversation, have we? So what did we talk about that night?"

"Two things stand out in my mind. How much you love Frankie and the times in your life when you were always the runner-up."

"No wonder we talked so long. I know you thought I was exaggerating about the runner-up part but it's true. I never won any award when I was young or in high school and college either. I was pretty disappointed when I wasn't crowned the "Penny Princess" at age 5. Fortunately I got over that traumatic defeat and wasn't emotionally scarred for life. Not too sure if my mom has gotten over it though! I can hear you laughing by the way, Beth!"

"Yeah, I hope you're happy. I'm laughing so hard I just spilled coffee on my keyboard."

"I bet you're waiting for me to say something profound and philosophical now, aren't you? Something along the lines that being runner-up all the time helped shape my character. If you think we're capable of talking seriously for a few minutes without cracking up, I could enlighten you with some true feelings. Are you ready or are you still wiping off your keyboard?"

"I'm ready. Let's hear it!"

"Maybe being the runner-up is what has kept me humble my whole life. Had I been a winner, maybe I would have been arrogant and not touched by the underdogs in life. I've always been able to put myself in their shoes because I feel their pain, disappointments and hurt."

"You really don't think you're the extraordinary woman you are, do you?"

"I'm proud of what I do but I don't feel like it's extraordinary or unique. I see an opportunity and I go for it. I relish it. I have faith in myself and my decisions. I've met people along the way who are paralyzed by the fear of challenges and changes in their lives. It's kryptonite for me. It fuels my mind and actually makes my heart race with excitement."

"You know this is going in the book exactly as you've said it, don't you?"

"I hope it comes across to the reader in a good way because I really believe what I've said."

"I know you do, my friend. You have no idea what a 'teacher' you are."

"Beth, when we finish the book, I'm really going to miss these marathon conversations."

"Me too, Shelly."

~ ~ ~

The Runner-up Continued

Beth, after we hung up last night I was reminiscing about my childhood and I realized I forgot to tell you about another big moment in my life when I was the runner-up which began to feel like my calling. Whether it was the Penny Princess Pageant or the Campus Queen Pageant, I was always the runner-up.

What saved me emotionally was that I was always the winner in Mom and Dad's eyes and no matter what, they were always proud of me and my sisters. They made us feel good about "losing" and that is something few parents ever master. If not for them, I think I would have believed I didn't ever deserve to win. The one time they really were there for me was when I was up for the Matzoh Ball Queen Contest. For a short, svelte (nicer than the word plump back then) Jewish girl there are other honors you want to strive for but this was something I wanted because it was all about selling tickets. Whoever could sell the most tickets to the event won. That seemed simple enough and I knew this title would be mine. As a matter of fact, my date was the coordinator of the entire event and it was no secret throughout the many weeks leading up to this exciting day that Shelly Weiner would soon be crowned THE MATZOH BALL QUEEN! I had sold the most tickets.

Mom and Dad were so proud and as always, they were prepared to make this special for me. The event would take place in the evening and at the end of the night after the crowning, the tradition was to have the 'after party' at the winner's house. We had a huge basement in our home and that always seemed to be where everyone gravitated so it was an obvious choice that my party would be at the Weiners' house. Mom and Dad spent the week leading up to it buying food, drinks, desserts, games, music and decorations. They were ready and so was I!

The big announcement was scheduled for 9 o'clock. There were five of us gals and our dates on the stage; as I looked out over the crowd of hundreds, I could see my family taking up the first two rows so they could be there to congratulate me and have the best view of the crowning. As my date, the event coordinator, walked up to the microphone I heard the words: "And the winner is…" Wait, it is not Shelly! That can't be right! He just called out the name of my supposed best friend and neighbor! How could it NOT be me?

Apparently my friend's parents loved her as much as my parents loved me and at the last minute, they bought all the remaining tickets so their daughter would be crowned. She acted shocked but it was nothing close to the looks on the faces of my entire extended family- sisters, aunts, uncles, cousins, close friends and neighbors. Then the real shock came as she made her acceptance speech. She said that she was so overwhelmed and since her father had hemorrhoids, he was not able to put together a party; so there would be an "AFTER PARTY AT THE WEINERS!" Yes, Mom and Dad, my sisters and I had one big party for the winner - and I was the runner-up!

~ ~ ~

Crazy in Love

I got up very early this morning; I couldn't sleep because I had too much to do. I tried to cough quietly, dim the lights to find my contact lenses and muffle the five loud beeps of the coffee pot. I was hoping not to wake Frankie but my efforts were futile. I feel like he has an auto sensor on me and anytime I move, get up or turn over, he is wide awake to make sure I'm all right. That's when he asks, "Are you okay, baby?"

After working on the computer for a few hours (with him working at his desk behind me), I kissed him goodbye (two kisses-always) and went to the gym for my run. I did it quickly and skipped my usual workout because I was eager to get back home to write more of my book. I called Frankie on the way home to see where he was and what he was doing.

He told me what he'd gotten done (keep in mind it was only one hour since I saw him) and we talked as I drove home. He said he was going to the printer, the Post Office, the bank and then to Office Depot to pick up supplies we needed. As I drove into our subdivision, I glanced over at the pool area where our mailboxes are located and saw Frankie's car. My heart started pounding faster and as I glanced to the right, I saw him with his arm extended high in the air waving to me. I was SO excited to see him so I started honking the horn and waving like a maniac out the sunroof.

I called him as I pulled into our driveway to say how great it was seeing him. He said the same thing and then we talked a few more moments while I pulled in the garage. I told him I loved him and to make sure not to text while driving and pay attention to the road. (I know he is 48 years old and knows all this already). He told me to make sure to close the garage door all the way and lock the doors (even though we are in a guarded, gated community). He said he'd bring home lunch so we could take a break from work and eat together.

As I sat down at my computer to type, I realized how quiet the house was. I had the windows open so I could hear the sprinklers in back and the birds in front but I couldn't hear Frankie. How crazy- I missed him! Then I realized I am not crazy- I am just crazy in love!

~ ~ ~

Strength in Sharing

Shelly, I just finished listening to one of the radio programs you cohost with Stacey Schieffelin each Thursday morning on Toginet.com. I love the logo on your website: 'Strength in Sharing…make each moment matter.' You've done a wonderful job bringing in such highly esteemed professionals who provide women with so much self-help information. I can hear your enthusiasm and determination to inspire others to live life to the fullest in spite of any obstacles.

I can't help but smile when you're connecting with people. The women who call in end up feeling like they've known you for years. I can empathize. I felt the same way after our first phone conversation. I'll never forget your saying that night, "I think we're going to make great partners in writing my story, Beth."

We've become more than partners, haven't we? We've become wonderful friends. You mentioned last week that you felt "sad and happy about the book ending." I do as well but the book will never end as we join forces in the months and years ahead to speak to audiences and share your messages.

My favorite part of the book is when you stepped forward and said, "I'll help George." That really says it all about you, Shelly Maguire. You care about others, make them feel important and give them hope when faced with adversity. You are a champion to all whose lives you've touched. Now it's time for you to end your book with a powerful message people will never forget.

Your partner always,

Beth

~ ~ ~

Strength

When we are born, we are each given a finite amount of time on this earth, some shorter, some longer. Certain circumstances are out of our control. We cannot choose our families and I thank God that I was blessed with one that was wonderful and supportive. We cannot wish away a disease, save a failing marriage or bring back a lost friend or loved one.

Other situations are put before us to either seize or pass by. The business associations we form, the friendships we cultivate and the people we choose to love and spend our lives with influence who we are and the quality of our existence. We can either say "I want this opportunity, I want this thing, I want this person," or we can say "It's just too difficult, I'm too sick, I'm not smart enough, I'm not attractive enough, I'll surely fail."

Has CF affected my life? Of course. Have there been times when I've felt sorry for myself or thought that it was all so unfair? Absolutely. I have never known life without this disease and I do not know what person I would be without it. So as much as I pray for a cure, I also realize that it has made me who I am today. As of now, I'm waiting for my next pulmonary function test to see if my lungs have stabilized or are still in a declining pattern. I will eventually have to make a decision about whether or not to treat the abscesses bacteria which may be causing more problems (aside from my CF). I realize that one day I may not have the physical strength I have now and that no matter how badly my mind wants to run, it may be a physical impossibility. That scares me and keeps me motivated to keep running now. I am thankful that for now I feel good!

There have recently been so many new developments in CF-related drugs that the outlook is very encouraging for future generations. I secretly and selfishly pray it is in my lifetime. That is why I am dedicated to help "spread the word" what life with CF is really like and work hard to help the Cystic Fibrosis Foundation raise money for research.

There are many people besides me who face difficulties and challenges or who just feel different. My desire is that sharing my story and my life will offer inspiration and be a testament to the belief that something attempted and failed is a still a victory while something not attempted and regretted is a defeat. I want people to say "If she can do it, so can I." The wonderful thing about dreams and hopes is that they are not the exclusive right of the rich, the powerful, the lucky or the healthy. They're for everyone, and whether they are achieved or not, they can be altered and made anew at any point in life or at any age.

Too often we focus on the negatives in our lives and fail to realize that with work and will-power that negative can be channeled and redirected to make us stronger and eventually become a positive. If I have learned one thing in this life, it is that I don't want to live for today, I want to live for tomorrow even if tomorrow is the last day. I want to keep Dancing in the Storm.

Also by Beth Huffman

Run, Amy, Run!

Awesome Andrea